The DREAM BOOK

MEG WOLITZER

The Dream Book

GREENWILLOW BOOKS
New York

Library of Congress Cataloging-in-Publication Data
Wolitzer, Meg.
The dream book.
Summary: When eleven-year-old Claudia, living
alone with her mother, meets tough Danger Roth,
the two girls start sharing strange dreams in
which Claudia's missing father sends her
cryptic messages.
[1. Dreams—Fiction.
2. Extrasensory perception—Fiction.
3. Fathers and daughters—Fiction.
4. Single-parent family—Fiction]
I. Title.
PZ7.W8338Dr 1986   [Fic]   86-305
ISBN 0-688-05148-0

FOR JESSE GREEN
with gratitude

The DREAM BOOK

1

*T*here was a new girl in the building, and her name was Danger Roth. Claudia had seen her a few times before in the elevator but had never said hello. One day, when Claudia was heading downstairs to take her dog, Cupcake, out for a walk, there was that girl again. She was leaning against the back wall of the elevator. She had straight black hair that fell in her eyes.

"Hey," she said, when Claudia got on. "What's your name?"

1

"Claudia Lemmon," she answered. Cupcake began to sniff the new girl's feet.

"My name's Danger Roth," the girl said. "I've seen you before. We just moved in last week. Eighteen C."

"Four I," said Claudia as coolly as possible.

They got out at the bottom and went their separate ways. Cupcake yanked Claudia over to his favorite tree, and Danger Roth hailed a taxi in front of the building and it zoomed off.

That night at dinner Claudia's mother was circling help wanted ads in the newspaper, and Claudia sat at the table, just thinking about Danger. What a great name, she thought. I wish my name were something wonderful like that.

"How does this sound, honey?" her mother asked. "'Intelligent woman wanted to appear in art films. Must be worldly.'"

"Mom!" said Claudia. "That means you have to be nude!"

Her mother looked at the ad again. "Oh, yes, I guess you're right," she said. "Oh well. I thought they meant *art*, like something interesting that doesn't make sense. You know, an experimental film."

It constantly amazed Claudia how innocent her mother was. Claudia often had to tell her what things meant. She hadn't always been this way, Claudia thought. Sometimes she remembered her mother from the year before, when she was married

2

to Claudia's father and was much happier. She remembered the way her father used to sing songs to them in the evenings, songs that he had written at work, when he was supposed to be selling insurance.

"Oh, babe," his songs usually began, "you are so fine. I wanna find a way to make you mine. . . ."

He was a bald man in a dark business suit, but he liked to sing like a country-western singer. He would come home from work, loosen his tie, and pick up his guitar. Other fathers wanted a glass of beer and a newspaper when they came home each night, but not Claudia's father.

"Insurance salesman by day," he would say, "country and western music star by night!"

Then he would sing until Claudia's mother came in and told him that dinner was ready.

After a while he began drifting off at work, sitting and writing songs when he was supposed to be doing other things. One day he got into trouble and was fired. He came home and said, "Well, I've lost my job, but maybe it's a blessing in disguise. Now we can all travel around the country, and I can audition for the *Grand Ole Opry*. We'll get ourselves a trailer. We'll leave on the weekend!"

"Wait a minute, Murray," said Claudia's mother. "We can't take Claudia out of school. She's happy there. And I love our apartment and all our friends."

They argued long into the night, and Claudia had to put a pillow over her head to sleep. In the morning she woke up and walked into her parents' bedroom. Her father was packing a suitcase. "Where are you going, Dad?" she asked, and he sat down on the bed and explained that he had to leave for a while and strike out on his own.

"You sound like one of your songs, Murray," said Claudia's mother, coming into the bedroom. "You can't live your life like that."

But he would not change his mind. That afternoon he took off, carrying his suitcase, and didn't come back. Nearly nine months passed, and they still hadn't heard a word from him. Now Claudia's mother was looking for a job. Every day she went through the help wanted section and went for interviews, but so far nothing good had come up. If she didn't get a job soon, she said, they might have to move to a smaller apartment.

This made Claudia extremely sad. She loved the apartment and had lived there ever since she was born. It was located on Central Park West in New York City, and the windows in the living room looked out over the wide, quiet street. She didn't think any other place would be half as nice.

But these days things were falling apart in the apartment: The couch had started to sag in the middle, and one of the lamps kept blinking on and off when Claudia was trying to do her homework. Claudia had read lots of books about families that were so poor that the children had to be sent to foster homes.

4

"Don't be ridiculous," her mother said. "We're not *that* poor. We'll manage."

During the day, while her mother looked for work, Claudia went to the Grayfield School. Sometimes she felt useless, sitting there in class making dioramas and doing equations. She could have been out making money, she thought, but her mother told her to keep her mind on her schoolwork.

After her father had moved out, Claudia spent most of her time with her mother. They cooked dinner together, or watched TV, or played Monopoly. Claudia had drifted away from most of her friends in school. She had too much on her mind these days. Stephanie Hunt accused her of being stuck-up, but she just didn't understand.

When Claudia met Danger Roth, she knew that she wanted to be her friend, and she wasn't sure why. Maybe it was Danger's name or the tough way Danger stood at the back of the elevator, as though she owned the place. Whatever the reason, Claudia began to ride the elevator up and down one Saturday afternoon, hoping they would see each other again. She did this for half an hour, but no Danger. On the ninth floor Mrs. Jacoby got on.

"Hello, little one," she said. "Any word from that father of yours?"

"No," said Claudia.

On the fifteenth floor Molly Harding and her cello got on. Molly was a cellist with the New York Harmonia Orchestra, even though she was only eleven. She was always being interviewed in the newspaper.

"Hi, Molly," said Claudia.

"Hi, Claudia," said Molly.

"Where are you going?" asked Claudia.

"To practice," said Molly.

"Oh," said Claudia. "Don't you ever do anything else?"

"Well yes," said Molly. "I go out to buy new strings sometimes for my cello. Or else I go to a master class."

"Gee," said Claudia, "what variety."

"It's not bad," Molly said defensively. "The orchestra is going on a tour of the Soviet Union soon, and I already have a plane ticket."

The doors opened then, and Molly got off, lugging her cello behind her.

After another hour of riding up and down, Claudia was convinced that Danger wasn't going to show. Just for the heck of it Claudia rode the elevator up to the penthouse. The doors opened, and in walked Dr. Byrd. The doctor was an elderly woman with black hair pulled tightly back from her forehead. Her face was very pale, and she usually wore dark colors. She had moved into the building only a few weeks earlier.

"Good day," said Dr. Byrd.

Claudia, as usual, was tongue-tied. "Hi," she whispered. If Claudia's mother had been around, she would have told Claudia that she was being very rude.

Claudia tried to smile at Dr. Byrd now. They rode downstairs together, and Claudia got off on her own floor and went back home. Where, she wondered, was Danger Roth?

All that night, as she lay in bed, she thought about Danger. Cupcake climbed in with her and licked her face, then fell asleep at the foot of the bed. Claudia had a very strange dream. She dreamed that she was somewhere out in a boat, in the sea, and the water was filled with teenagers. They all were swimming around, having a party, and shouting and laughing. When Claudia woke up in the morning, she got dressed, told her mother she had an errand to run, and then she went upstairs to the eighteenth floor. She rang the bell of apartment 18C, and in a minute the door opened, and Danger was standing there in her pajamas.

"Hey," said Danger, not at all surprised. "I was going to come to your apartment."

Claudia walked in. "I don't even know why I'm here, really," she said. "I just wanted to come. I haven't even eaten breakfast. I was having a weird dream."

"Me, too," said Danger. "I'll get you something to eat."

The apartment was filled with boxes that hadn't yet been unpacked. "I think I can find a cereal bowl

7

somewhere in the mess," said Danger. "I'd ask my mother, but she's taking a shower, and my father's in the darkroom." Danger looked around for a few minutes and finally came up with a bowl and a spoon. She poured out some granola, and Claudia sat on a step stool and ate.

"How did you get your name?" Claudia asked between mouthfuls.

"It's a long story," said Danger. "Do you really want to hear it?"

"Yes," said Claudia, "please."

So Danger leaned back against the wall, closed her eyes, and said, "When my mother was pregnant with me, my parents were on a safari in Africa. My mother and father are both photographers, and they were on assignment. Anyway, everything was going fine, and my mother thought they would finish up their work, then come back to New York and have me, but one day there was a giant stampede of buffalo, and my parents knew that something was wrong. The buffalo looked terrified, and it turned out that they were being chased by a pack of wild jungle tigers. Most of the photographers hid in the trees, where they knew the tigers couldn't find them. My father helped my mother climb up into a giant uzami tree, which is a very common tree in the region. My mother was eight and a half months pregnant, and she and my father stayed in that tree for four days. Two tigers circled the tree just below, waiting for them to climb down. Luckily the uzami tree bears a wonderful fruit, called uzu, which is green and sweet and has enough juice and pulp in it so my parents didn't starve to death."

Claudia just sat listening, her eyes wide.

"Finally," said Danger, "a rescue team from the Peace Corps came and captured the wild tigers, and then my mother, who had just gone into labor, was rushed in the direction of the hospital. She gave birth in the jeep. My parents named me Danger, because that was what I was certainly born in. They were thinking of naming me Uzu, but I'm glad they didn't."

"Wow," said Claudia. "That's incredible. I hate my name. It's so boring! It doesn't have any story attached to it. You're so lucky, Danger."

All of a sudden there were footsteps, and someone came into the room. It was a tall woman with a towel wrapped around her head. "Mindy," she said, "I asked you to help unpack."

Claudia looked around her, confused.

"Uh, okay, Mom," said Danger. "I will, I will. This is my friend Claudia."

"Hello," said the woman. "You'll excuse my appearance."

Then she turned and walked back down the hall.

Mindy! Why had she called her Mindy? Claudia wondered. Had Danger been telling the truth about her name? For the first time it occurred to Claudia that she might have been lying. It was all very strange.

"Anyway," said Danger, obviously anxious to change the subject, "tell me your dream. Then I'll tell you mine."

So Claudia told her the dream about the teenagers swimming around in the sea.

"Hmmmmm," said Danger. "That's really interesting. I had a strange dream last night, too, as I said, and usually I don't remember my dreams. Usually I just remember a color. Like I'll dream beige, but that's about it. This was my dream," she said. "I was running down a long corridor, following a monster with four eyes. But it wasn't a bad monster. It was a good one, and for some reason I really wanted to talk to it. Then I woke up. And I was just about to come over to your apartment when you showed up."

The two girls just sat there. "A teenage sea and a four-eyed monster," said Danger. She leaned her head in her hands, and her black hair covered her face. She looked as though she were meditating. All of a sudden she snapped up, her finger in the air.

"Wait a minute!" she said. "You're not going to believe it! *A teen sea!*" she said. *"Four eye!"*

"Yeah," said Claudia. "So?"

Danger stood up and looked triumphant. Her face was flushed. "What apartment do you live in, Claudia?" she asked.

"Four I," said Claudia. "So?"

"And I live in eighteen C," said Danger. "Get it?

We had dreams about each other's apartment! You had a dream about a teen sea—eighteen C! I had a dream about four eye—four I, the number of your apartment! We were destined to meet!"

It took Claudia a moment for this really to sink in, but when it did, she felt the most wonderful, peculiar shiver go all the way down her spine.

2 °₀°

*T*he dreams convinced them that they were fated to be friends. Danger wanted to seal their friendship in blood, but Claudia said no. Still, she was excited, and when she went home that afternoon, she told her mother all about Danger. She didn't mention the dreams; they were a secret.

"She sounds like a very interesting girl," said her mother. "I'm glad you're making friends again. I'm certainly not enough companionship for an eleven-year-old."

Claudia and Danger had decided that they would think about each other right before they went to sleep that night. If they thought about each other hard enough, then perhaps they would dream about each other again. As Claudia lay in bed, she pictured Danger's straight black hair and her scowling face. When she finally fell asleep, she slept straight through the night, and in the morning she didn't remember any of her dreams. Her mind was as clear and bright as a coin.

She went off to school, and as she was going down in the elevator, there was Danger, also heading off to school. Danger went to the Shipwell School, which was five blocks in the opposite direction. "I've never heard of that school," said Claudia.

"It's for troubled youngsters," said Danger. "That's what it said in the brochure. I took a peek at it when my parents weren't around."

"Why do you have to go there?" asked Claudia.

Danger shrugged. "Because," she said. "Because everyone at my old school was stupid and nobody understood me. They said that I had to go somewhere for 'children like me.'"

"So, are there children like you at your new school?" asked Claudia.

"Not really," Danger said. "Miss Cotner said that I am a unique individual. Mostly, everyone goes into the bathroom and smokes. Sometimes they wreck the whole place and get suspended. Once in a while someone is arrested for stealing hubcaps. Everyone there thinks they're so tough."

13

So do you, Claudia wanted to say, but she didn't. She kept silent. She liked Danger's toughness; it was so unlike herself. Claudia was scared of a lot of things. She was scared of the darkness in the apartment at night. She felt afraid that if a burglar broke in, she and her mother wouldn't be able to protect themselves. Not that her father had been particularly strong or anything, but for some reason she had always felt safe with him around. And she was scared of certain older kids in school. She was also scared of the snake that was kept in a tank in her classroom and scared of certain episodes of *The Twilight Zone*. She just bet that Danger wouldn't be scared of any of those things.

Every day after school she and Danger had a snack at one or the other's apartment.

Danger's mother and father both were photographers. Most of the people whom they photographed were children. They took baby pictures of infants sprawled out naked on bear rugs or birthday pictures of twin boys in matching outfits. Sometimes Danger led clients into the big white studio. "This way," she would say, leading a scared child and his mother down the long hallway.

Usually Danger and Claudia shut themselves into Danger's bedroom. It was a small room filled with junk: rocks; seashells; books; baseball caps. Each item had a story behind it. The rock was found on Friday the thirteenth and was a superstition rock.

14

The seashell was from ancient Greece. The books had belonged to a boy who had vanished.

Claudia's own room was very boring and neat; it held a fish tank, a bed which she made every day, and a bookshelf with all her favorites lined up. Nothing in the room was very old or had belonged to anyone remotely famous or dead. Most of the things had been bought new for her by her parents.

"I don't have any mysteries in my life," Claudia told Danger. "Except the mystery of my father."

Danger perked up. "What mystery of your father?" she asked. "Tell me all the details."

So Claudia told her about how her father had taken off and hadn't returned. She went through the whole story, and it made her sad thinking about it again, but Danger didn't seem impressed.

"Oh, *that* kind of disappeared," she said. "That's nothing special. It happens all the time. Half the kids in my school have divorced parents."

Claudia looked down. "They're not divorced exactly," she said in a tiny voice. "My mother didn't want my father to go. It's not the same thing."

"There's no big difference," Danger said, as though she knew everything.

It was times like these that made Claudia want to slam out of Danger's room and never come back. Sometimes Danger was so insensitive! But she never argued with her. A moment after Claudia felt bad, they would do something else, and Claudia would feel good again. She would forget all about her father for the time being and play Parcheesi.

Claudia and Danger had been friends for almost a week, but still they hadn't had any other interesting dreams. "I don't understand it," said Danger. "I could have sworn that it was a sign of some kind, telling us to be friends. But maybe I was wrong."

Danger believed in those kinds of things: superstitions, and witchcraft, and good and evil. Claudia wasn't sure how she felt about any of it. Mostly she had never paid attention to that sort of thing. But after the first dream she had been a little shaken up.

Claudia continued to spend most of her time with Danger and forgot about the dreams until one night, three days later, she had another dream.

In this dream she and Danger were sitting in a waiting room, and suddenly out came a nurse, beckoning them inside. For some reason they were terrified, and they fled out into the hall.

Claudia woke up in the early morning, yelling, "Please leave us alone! Please!"

Her mother was standing over the bed, shaking her awake. "Honey," her mother kept saying, "it was only a dream. It's okay."

Claudia felt upset by the dream all day. At school she kept thinking about it and could barely concentrate on class. When she got home at three o'clock, Danger was waiting for her out front, under the awning of the building.

16

"Did you have a terrible day?" Danger asked. "No concentration?"

"How did you know?" asked Claudia.

"Because I had the same problem," said Danger. "I figured that you did, too. I dreamed about us last night."

"Okay," said Claudia. "You tell me yours first."

"Well," said Danger, "we were sitting in a waiting room. I think I was reading *National Geographic* or something, because there were all these pictures of African warriors—"

"Get to the important part," said Claudia impatiently.

"Well," said Danger, "all of a sudden an evil nurse came out of the office—"

"And beckoned to us, and we ran away, screaming!" broke in Claudia.

"How did you know?" asked Danger, astonished.

"Because I dreamed the exact same thing," said Claudia, and once again she felt that shiver go up and down her spine.

"Something is definitely going on here," said Danger. "I think we should keep a journal about our dreams. At my school we all have to keep journals. We're supposed to write down things like 'I stole that bicycle because . . .' or 'I hit that old lady because . . .'"

"Let's go out and buy a notebook," said Claudia. She and Danger walked to the store and wandered for a long time down the narrow aisles before they found just the right notebook. It was very big and was a pale pink color. The pages had no lines on them. That was good, said Danger, in case they wanted to draw pictures of their dreams. They both loved to draw.

As they were leaving the store, Claudia heard a familiar voice behind her, talking to the salesboy.

"Do you have any lead pencils?" asked the voice. "The old-fashioned kind?"

It was Dr. Byrd. Claudia turned and quickly glanced at her. As usual, Dr. Byrd was bundled up in a heavy coat. Today she wore a thick black fur hat on her head. It just sat on top of her hair, like an animal.

"Who's that?" whispered Danger. "Do you know her?"

"She's pretty new in the building," said Claudia. "Her name is Dr. Byrd. She's a little weird."

They left the store, but Danger was still interested in talking about Dr. Byrd. "What kind of doctor is she?" Danger persisted.

"I don't know," said Claudia. "But she *is* creepy. She wears all those weird fur hats, but it's not only that. It's just a feeling I have—I can't really explain it. Sometimes I get these feelings—what's the word?—*intuition*. That's a word my mother uses a lot. She says I have good intuition about things. Like those ads she keeps answering in the paper. I always tell her when I think they're advertising some terrible job, like for a stripper or a sword swallower, but she never believes me. She has to go see for herself. Sometimes it takes her three subways to get to the interview, and when she comes home, she says, 'Claudia, I should have trusted your intuition.'"

"I think you're psychic," Danger said quietly.

"I am not! I'm not crazy!" said Claudia.

"I said *psychic*, not *psychotic*," said Danger. "*Psychic* means you know certain things without being told. You just have a feeling about them. Sometimes you can dream things, and they come true. Or else your dreams give you certain messages that you're supposed to follow. Only psychic people have dreams like that. I'm the same way, Claudia," she said. "That's why we were destined to be friends. That's why my parents moved here. Just so you and I could meet. It was in the stars." She paused. "You know, that last dream," she mused. "Maybe it had something to do with Dr. Byrd."

Claudia was skeptical, but still, she liked hearing Danger sound so excited. She lost some of her toughness. She moved her hands a lot when she talked now.

"Let's go up to my apartment," said Claudia. "We can start our dream book."

They went up to the fourth floor and let themselves in with Claudia's key. There was a note taped to the refrigerator, which read: "Honey, I am out at yet another job interview. Will be back by dinner.

Cross your fingers for me. Please take out the pot roast when you get home. Love and kisses, Mom."

Claudia took the leftover pot roast out of the refrigerator and dropped it onto the counter. Then she and Danger ate a few cookies and sat down at the kitchen table with their dream book.

Claudia took some Magic Markers out of her knapsack. "What should we write on the cover?" she asked.

"How about 'The Dream Book'?" said Danger.

Claudia agreed, and she and Danger wrote the words across the pink cover, each of them taking turns writing a letter. They used every color of Magic Marker that Claudia had.

"It should have an illustration, too," said Claudia. "How about a girl in a bed?"

"I don't know," said Danger. "Can't we come up with something more mysterious?"

In the end they decided on a drawing of a cloud with a question mark underneath.

"It looks symbolic," said Danger.

Claudia had to admit that the drawing looked good. They opened to the first page of the notebook and wrote "Dream #1," and they described what had happened in the first set of dreams. Then Claudia drew a picture of her teenage sea, and Danger drew a picture of the four-eyed monster. On the next page they wrote "Dream #2," and together they drew the doctor's office and the long corridor. They wrote a paragraph about the dream, and when they were done, they closed the book.

"Who's going to keep it?" asked Danger.

"It doesn't matter," said Claudia. "We could take turns if you want."

"Fine," said Danger. "Just don't run off with it for good."

How could she even think something like that? Claudia wondered. She guessed that it was because everyone in Danger's school was tough and stole things, so Danger didn't trust anybody, not even her friends.

"You can take it home with you today," Claudia offered.

"Fine," said Danger.

Then the front door opened, and Claudia's mother walked in. "Forget the pot roast!" she called out. "We're going out to dinner to celebrate!" She came into the kitchen with her coat on.

"Celebrate what, Mom?" asked Claudia.

"Your mother is now officially employed," she said.

Claudia jumped up and hugged her mother. "That's terrific, Mom!" she said. "I'm so happy for you!"

"Yeah, congrats, Ms. L," said Danger.

"Thank you, Danger," said Claudia's mother. "Don't you girls even want to know where I'll be working?"

"Tell us," said Claudia.

"I am now an employee of the Anglo-American School of the English Language," she said. "I am a tutor of foreign students who want to learn to speak English."

"That's wonderful, Mom," said Claudia.

Danger stood up, quickly sliding the dream book into her satchel. "I've got to get going," she said.

"Bye," said Claudia. "Take good care of you know what."

After Danger had left, Claudia's mother said, "What was that about?"

"Nothing," said Claudia.

"Oh," said her mother. "Well, in that case, let's go out to eat. I'm starving. Want Chinese?"

"Yeah!" said Claudia, because Chinese food was her absolute favorite kind.

So she put her coat back on, and she and her mother went out the door of the apartment, leaving the pot roast behind on the counter.

3 ⁘

*T*he dreams were appearing with a strange regularity: one every nine days. As soon as they realized this, they relaxed during the in-between times and didn't try to think hard about each other before going to sleep. Claudia was involved in a big project for school; it was a dramatization of the life of Harriet Tubman. She and two other partners in the project drew straws. Stephanie Hunt got to be Harriet Tubman. Claudia was Slave Driver No. 2. It wasn't a very interesting part. Still, she practiced it with her mother in the evenings. Her mother played the other parts:

HARRIET: I think I'm going to try to find a way to help end slavery and free the black people once and for all.

SLAVE DRIVER NO. 1 *(entering):* Hey, what are you doing in there? I told you to blow out that candle and go to bed! I won't have you staying up at night, teaching yourself to read and write! You've got to be up early in the morning to work. Shut off that light!

SLAVE DRIVER NO. 2 [Claudia]: Yeah, and we're not kidding! *(Exits.)*

"No part is too small," said her mother. "There are only small actors, Claudia."

"Yeah, yeah," muttered Claudia.

One afternoon she went down in the elevator to walk Cupcake, and she ran into Danger, who was going out to mail a letter.

"Hey there," Danger said.

"Hey," said Claudia.

"What's new in the four-eyed monster house?" asked Danger.

"Nothing," said Claudia. "What's new in the teen-age sea?"

Danger smiled. "Not too much," she said. "My parents are photographing triplets today. Three five-

24

year-old girls named Heather, Holly, and Ivy." She made a face. "I'm dying for a cigarette," she said.

"Danger," said Claudia, "you can't smoke. You're only eleven."

"So what?" said Danger. "When I'm bored, I like to smoke. I have to find someplace really private to do it; that's the only problem. My parents would kill me if they knew. Want to come?" she asked.

"I have to walk the dog," said Claudia. "And smoking is really dangerous. You know that."

"Have it your own way," said Danger. "I'll just go off by myself and have a Marlboro."

"Where are you going to get one?" asked Claudia.

"You'll see," said Danger.

When they got to the first floor, they walked through the lobby together, and Danger went over to the doorman and said, "Hey, Frank, do you have a cigarette I could bum off you?"

Frank looked horrified. "No way, little lady," he said. "You think I want to lose my job? Why don't you get some candy cigarettes instead?" He chuckled softly to himself, then suddenly lunged forward to open the door. He swung it wide, and the wind blew in with a great whoosh. In came Dr. Byrd.

"Thank you, Frank," she said.

Claudia tried to hide behind a plant, but it was too late; the doctor had already seen her.

"Good afternoon," Dr. Byrd said.

"Hi," said Claudia, looking down at her shoes. Cupcake yanked Claudia over in the direction of the door, and Claudia was relieved. She didn't want to have an awkward conversation with Dr. Byrd. What would they have talked about? Tongue depressors? Yearly checkups?

Outside, Danger was eager to talk about Dr. Byrd. "She seems like a fishy character to me," she said. "I bet *she* was the doctor in our dreams. You know," she said, leaning close to Claudia's ear, "these dreams are here for a purpose. I think they're trying to tell us to *do* something, to take some action. We can't just keep ignoring them; we've got to figure them out. Dr. Byrd seems like a reasonable place to start."

"So what do you think we should do?" asked Claudia.

"I'm not sure," she said. She thought about it for a moment. "Hey, I've got an idea," she said. "We can pretend that you've fainted and bring you up to Dr. Byrd's office, and when she turns her back, we can look around."

Claudia immediately said no. "My mother would get very worried," she said. "I'm sure Dr. Byrd would mention the whole thing to her. My mother can't even bear it if I have the flu; she's very over-protective. I don't think it's a very good idea, Danger."

"Yeah, maybe you're right," said Danger. "Well," she said, "I'm sure we'll come up with something when the right time comes."

26

"How will we know when the right time comes?" asked Claudia.

"We just will," said Danger. "It will be a part of our intuition."

Cupcake was pulling Claudia urgently toward a fire hydrant. "I've got to take care of him," she said. "I'll talk to you later, Danger."

"Don't forget," said Danger. "Tonight is the ninth night since the last dream. I think we're in for a good one."

"But we haven't even solved the last one yet," said Claudia. "They're just going to start piling up."

"Relax," said Danger. "It will all work out."

But Claudia wasn't so sure. "We have a lot to do each day," she said. "I don't even know when we're going to find the time to think about the dreams. We both happen to go to school, and then, of course, we have homework."

"Relax," Danger repeated, and then she walked away.

Claudia took the dog for a good long walk around the block. When she got back, there was no sign of Danger. She peered into a narrow alleyway between buildings and saw a young girl leaning against the wall, smoking. The smoke clouded the air around her, but still, Claudia could tell that it was Danger. She had somehow managed to find cigarettes. Leave it to Danger, Claudia thought, shaking her head.

That night, as expected, Claudia had the third

dream. In it a young girl was about to get on an airplane. Claudia stood at the gate, waving goodbye. She watched as the girl walked up the stairs to the plane, carrying a giant bowl of Jell-O. Claudia just stood watching, and then she woke up. It wasn't a dream that she understood. It didn't leave her feeling spooked, or happy, or uncomfortable. It was just a dream that didn't make too much sense, like most of her old dreams, before she had met Danger.

She began to think about other things. She had her week to plan out. On Thursday her school had the day off so the teachers could have a conference. She thought she would sleep late that day and maybe spend the afternoon in the park. She looked forward to being alone.

When she got home from school, Danger called. "I have a lot of work to do," Danger said, "so I figured we'd better discuss this third dream over the phone."

"Okay," said Claudia.

"It was pretty exciting, don't you think?" Danger asked.

Claudia's face fell. They had had entirely different dreams! Maybe the magic, if you could call it that, had worn off.

"My dream was boring," said Claudia. She told Danger the dream about the girl getting onto the airplane.

"Wait a minute," said Danger when Claudia was through. "I dreamed the next part of your dream!"

Her voice was excited. "I dreamed that this girl was walking up the ramp, carrying a bowl of Jell-O, and then I came up to her and yelled, 'Don't do it! Don't go!' She just stood there and looked at me for a long time. The stewardess stood at the top of the stairs, waiting for the girl to get on the plane. I just knew that if she went, something terrible would happen to her."

It occurred to them both that there were three different types of dreams. The first dream had concealed some hidden information, and each girl had the mirror image of the other's dream. The second set of dreams was exactly alike. And in the third type one girl started a dream, and the other one finished it.

"Who do you think the girl was?" asked Claudia.

"I don't know," said Danger. "I couldn't see her face."

"And what does the dream mean?" asked Claudia. "Are we supposed to do something about it? Maybe it's a message of some kind, and we can't figure it out, like the second dream. Maybe that plane was going to crash, and we could have done something to help." She thought for a moment. "Do you know anyone who's going on a plane trip?" she asked.

Danger thought about it. "No," she said. "Not that I can think of. My aunt Janice is taking a car trip to the Kentucky Derby this year, but that's about it."

"No offense, but I don't think we'd dream about that," said Claudia.

They couldn't think of anything, and finally they got too frustrated and talked about something else.

"I've got to go work," said Danger. "I need to prepare for Share and Reveal. It's my school's version of Show and Tell. What do you think I should bring in? My cockroach collection?"

"Why don't you talk about us?" Claudia asked. "Tell them about our dreams. Maybe they would understand."

"That's a thought," said Danger. "I was going to keep it a secret, but nobody in my class matters that much. It's a good idea. Hey!" she suddenly said. "Do you want to come to school with me on Thursday for Share and Reveal. Don't you have the day off?"

"Well yes," said Claudia.

"It would be great if you could come," said Danger. "That would show them."

"All right," said Claudia, "I'll do it." She was curious to see what Danger's school was really like.

They said goodbye then and hung up. Claudia went into the kitchen and started dinner. Her mother was away at training classes for her job every day, learning how to be a tutor of the English language. Pretty soon she would start to give lessons in the apartment.

Now Claudia just wandered around by herself, looking at things. There on top of the television set was her favorite photograph. It was a picture of Claudia and her parents standing on the beach, smiling at the camera. Her father had a little triangle of white lotion on his nose to protect it from the sun. Her mother and father were holding hands.

She thought about her father, tried to imagine where he might be. He could have been almost anywhere in the world. How could he have just left them like that? she wondered. She didn't know if she could ever forgive him. She didn't care what Danger thought; it was still a mystery to her.

The apartment was very peaceful in the late afternoon, but Claudia felt lonely. She set the table for dinner and went back to studying her meager part in the Harriet Tubman play. Sometimes she thought her whole life was going to be spent on the sidelines—Slave Driver No. 2! When would she ever be the center of attention? When would she ever stop being shy? Maybe if she spent more time with Danger, she would learn how to be assertive. Most of Claudia's friends were usually like Claudia: quiet, slightly timid, and straight-A students. She was never friends with the girls who were gymnasts, or cheerleaders, or tap-danced in the talent show at school. She was never friends with the girls in the sixth grade who already had boyfriends.

Claudia's mother came home at six, flushed and happy. "What a wonderful day I had!" she said. "All the people are so interesting! I think this job is going to change my life."

They sat down to dinner together at the big dining room table.

"You and Danger seem to be having lots of fun,"

said her mother. "What are you always whispering about?"

"Nothing," said Claudia. She and Danger had agreed not to talk about the dreams with their parents; it would only cause trouble. They knew that their parents would think the dreams were nonsense.

They ate dinner quietly, and Claudia's mother talked about her new job. Afterward they washed the dishes together, and Claudia went to sleep early. She had so much on her mind that she needed a break from her thoughts for a while.

The next day, after school had let out, she and Danger met in front of the building and went upstairs together. They ran into Molly Harding in the lobby. As usual, Molly was lugging her gigantic cello.

"Hi, Molly," said Claudia. "This is my friend Danger Roth. She just moved into the building."

Molly peered around the side of her cello case. "Hi," she said.

"Where are you off to now?" Claudia asked.

"To a lesson," Molly said. "We're all preparing for the big trip to Russia tomorrow. You know, I told you about it. We're going on a concert tour of the whole Soviet Union."

"Wait a minute," said Danger. "How are you getting there?"

"How do you think?" said Molly. "We're using our instruments as boats and sailing across the ocean."

"Be serious," said Danger.

"We're flying, of course," said Molly. She glanced at her wristwatch. "I'm going to be late," she said. "Professor Gronsky hates it when I'm late."

"Well, bye," said Claudia.

"*Wait* a minute," said Danger. "Claudia," she said, "maybe Molly is the girl in the dream going on the trip."

Molly looked puzzled. "Look," she said, "I have to go or I'll be late." Then she picked up her cello and continued to trudge across the lobby.

When she had gone out the door, Danger poked Claudia and said, "I swear, Claudia, I have a feeling about that girl. I think she's the one."

"Well, where's her bowl of Jell-O?" asked Claudia. "Just tell me that."

Danger thought for a long minute; then she snapped up, her finger in the air again. "It wasn't *Jell-O*, Claudia," she said. "That was just wordplay to clue us in. It wasn't Jell-O; it was a cello! Molly was carrying her cello onto the plane!"

"And we've got to stop her!" said Claudia.

Both girls raced down the hall and out into the street, where Molly Harding was still looking for a taxi. It had begun to rain.

"Molly!" Claudia shouted. "Molly, wait!"

Molly turned in annoyance. "What is it now?" she asked. "I have to get to my lesson."

The rain suddenly began to come down in a torrent. "Molly, we want to talk to you," said Claudia.

"I told you I can't," said Molly. "Sometimes,

Claudia Lemmon, you are just so *thick!* I have to get to my lesson, so leave me alone."

The rain was drenching the three of them, but they continued to stand in the street. It seemed that there was no way to get through to Molly Harding. Claudia was very worried; what if Molly went on the airplane and something terrible happened? She didn't even want to think about it.

She watched as Molly tried to hail a taxi in the pouring rain. It was coming down so hard that it was impossible to see the traffic; all that Claudia could see were headlights shining through the blur of water. She and Danger stood helplessly, watching as Molly Harding finally went off to her cello lesson. There was nothing to be done.

4

*T*he hijacking was on the news the next night at dinner. Claudia's knife and fork clattered to her plate.

"The New York Harmonia Orchestra was traveling to the Soviet Union for a concert tour," said the anchorman, "when their airplane was suddenly hijacked to Flavia, a small country near the Baltic Sea."

"Oh no," said Claudia and her mother at the same time.

Her mother stood up. "Molly must be on that plane!" she said. "I've got to call her parents. I'm sure they're worried sick!"

She went and dialed the Hardings' number. Claudia sat tensely at the table and listened.

"Yes, I see," her mother was saying. "Oh, yes, of course. . . . I can imagine, Sheila, I can certainly imagine. . . . My God, we were certainly worried for you. . . . Yes, indeed." Then she hung up.

"What did she say?" asked Claudia.

Claudia's mother smiled. "You're not going to believe this," she said. "That girl is very, very lucky. Last night she came down with the flu and *didn't go.* The orchestra had somebody sub for her."

Claudia was stunned. Didn't go? she thought. She kept remembering the way Molly had stood out there in the rain, being detained by Claudia and Danger. That was when she had probably caught the flu. Claudia and Danger were responsible for keeping Molly from going to the Soviet Union after all. Claudia couldn't get over it. The dream really had been telling them an important message. Later that night she and Danger had discussed it on the phone for hours, until their mothers yelled for them to get off.

The next day Claudia went to Share and Reveal at Danger's school. The front of the building was very ordinary, with red brick and barred windows. "I'm very nervous," said Claudia. "I've never done this before."

"Neither have I," said Danger. "But it will be interesting; I guarantee it."

They walked up the front steps; there was a group of kids hanging around outside, wearing matching leather vests. Across the back of each one was written the words "KILLER SHARKS."

"Hey," said Danger.

"Hey," said a gigantic boy. "How are you doing, Dange?"

"Okay," said Danger. "This is my friend Claudia."

"Hi, Claude," said the boy. "My name's Gruber."

"Hey, Grube," said another boy.

It seemed that all final syllables of people's names were dropped at this school. Claudia stood shyly on the steps, feeling uncomfortable in her thick coat and itchy hat. She felt like running away. Suddenly a piercing bell rang, and all the kids continued to sit there, as though they hadn't heard a thing.

"Want to play cards?" Gruber asked her.

"Cards?" she said. "Like crazy eights?"

"Hey, that's pretty funny," he said. "Dange, your friend here is pretty funny."

"Don't you have to go into class?" asked Claudia.

"All in good time, my pretty," said Gruber. "When they want me, they can come and get me."

As if on cue, the door suddenly swung open, and out walked a man with a crew cut and a suit and tie. "All right, you juvenile delinquents," he said. "Come on in. Didn't you hear that bell?"

"No, sir," said a chorus of voices. "It must have been broken or something."

"Well, get up, all of you, and come on inside," said the man. He began herding in everyone, even Claudia.

Inside, the hallways were dim and narrow. There was nothing tacked up on the walls. "It's not that they want it to be like a prison," Danger explained. "It's just that anytime someone puts something up, some jerk tears it down."

"Oh," said Claudia. Danger was walking quickly now, and Claudia tried to keep up with her. They went into a classroom at the end of the hall. The chairs were already formed into a big circle. Half the kids looked asleep. They sat on the chairs with their legs stretched out.

"Good morning, Danger," said the teacher, Miss Cotner. "This must be your friend Claudia, whom you told me about. Come in, please. We're about to start Share and Reveal. Janine, you can go first."

A tall, thin girl with frizzy blond hair stood up in the middle of the circle. "Share and Reveal," she said in a flat voice. "What I brought in for Share and Reveal is a trick about framing innocent people. My brother showed it to me. This is what you do: You go into a bank, and you go over to the place where they keep the withdrawal slips, and underneath one, on the carbon, you write 'This is a stickup. Give me all your money.' Then you place the slip back on top of the pile. Then you sit somewhere else in the bank, where you can watch the fun begin. Pretty soon somebody comes over to use a withdrawal slip, and they fill it out and bring it up to the counter, not knowing what's going on. It could even be a little old lady. She fills out the slip and hands it to the teller, and the teller rips off the carbon and sees what it says underneath. She presses a secret button underneath the counter, and in a minute the old lady is arrested. In the meantime, the kid who did the trick just sits across the room and watches the whole thing." The girl paused. "Well, that's all," she said.

Nobody seemed the least bit shocked. Claudia sat there with her mouth open, but everyone else just looked bored. "Well," said Miss Cotner, "that was fine, Janine, but it was really more *share* than *reveal*. Next time you might want to bring in some withdrawal slips to pass around, or else do a small re-enactment of the scene. But still, you were very articulate. I'll give you a B plus."

The girl sat down, satisfied.

"All right, Danger, you're next," said Miss Cotner.

Danger stood up in the center of the circle. "Okay, everybody," she said. "I've been having a very weird experience with my friend Claudia here." Then she told the story of the dreams and even the latest development involving Molly Harding. She had brought in the dream book, which she passed around in a circle so everyone could see.

"I also brought in Claudia, so you could see that I wasn't lying. The whole thing is completely authentic," said Danger.

"How do we know you didn't make it up?" asked a boy.

"You just have to take my word for it," said Danger, and at this, everybody laughed. Even Miss Cotner seemed to find it amusing.

"Claudia, tell them it's true," said Danger.

Claudia stood up. "It is," she said in a trembling voice. "Every word of it."

"What about the second dream?" asked a girl in a big, floppy hat. "It didn't lead to anything. How do you explain it?"

"We haven't figured it out yet," said Claudia, "although we have a hunch. We're working on it."

"Eventually we'll understand everything," said Danger. "One day it will all make sense to us, like a giant mystery."

A couple of kids snorted. "Oh, Danger, get off it," said another boy. "You don't tell the truth about *anything*. How are we supposed to believe you?"

"Yeah," said the girl in the hat. "Like the story about your name. That ridiculous story about your parents being international race car drivers and naming you that because you were born at the side of the racetrack, in the line of danger."

"We all know your real name is Mindy," said another girl.

"So what?" said Danger. "At least I have an imagination, unlike most of you jokers, who can just sit around and do nothing with your brains all day."

"Well, if you have such a vivid imagination," said Miss Cotner, "then it's possible that you're lying about the dreams. I'm afraid that I just don't believe you, Danger, and I'm going to have to give you a D for Share and Reveal."

Danger was furious. "Jeez," she said, "you can't win in this place." She turned to Claudia. "I guess you'd better go," she said. "Nobody around here believes us."

"But it's true," Claudia said to the class one last time, but everybody continued to smirk, and so she picked up her coat and hat and mittens and left.

When she got home, her mother was in the living room, talking to somebody. Claudia just assumed that Mrs. Flanagan from upstairs must be visiting, but when she listened closely, she was surprised.

"Very good," she heard her mother say. "Now let's try those verbs again, this time in the past tense."

"I comed into the room, and I seen the girl what sat on a chair," said a shy female voice.

"No," said Claudia's mother patiently. "It's 'I came into the room, and I saw the girl who sat in the chair.'"

"How can I remember such a thing?" said the woman. "It is impossible!"

41

Claudia peered into the living room. Her mother was sitting with a young woman who was wearing a long dress made of purple silk.

"Oh, here's my daughter, Claudia," said her mother. "Claudia, I would like you to meet Miss Neruda, my new pupil."

"Hello," said Claudia.

"Very pleaseful," said the woman, smiling shyly.

"Miss Neruda is from India," said Claudia's mother. "She has just moved here with her family and would like to learn English."

"That sounds nice," said Claudia. "Mom, can I have a Chips Ahoy!?"

"Yes, dear. I think there are a few left in the cookie jar," said her mother.

"Nice to meet you, Miss Neruda," Claudia said. She walked out of the living room, leaving them to their lesson. As she walked down the hall, she could hear Miss Neruda murmuring.

"Please, Mrs. Lemmon," she was saying. "What is Chipsahoy? Shall I learn the word?"

Claudia took a few cookies from the bottom of the jar and poured herself a glass of milk. She sat at the table, swinging her legs, the way she always did when she was thinking hard. She thought about the second dream, the unsolved one, and wondered if it really did have to do with Dr. Byrd. She thought that she and Danger ought to go up to the penthouse and check out Dr. Byrd's office.

That night she called Danger and suggested the idea to her. "Sounds good," said Danger. "When do you want to go?"

"How about tomorrow, after school?" said Claudia.

They agreed to meet, and then Claudia's mother began calling her, and she had to get off the telephone.

"What is it, Mom?" asked Claudia.

"Well, honey," said her mother, "we just haven't talked very much lately, and I feel bad about it. You're so busy with your friend Danger, and I'm wrapped up in my new job. Maybe we could spend some time together over the weekend."

"I'd like that," said Claudia, and she realized that she did miss her mother. She looked at her mother's kind, concerned face—the same blue eyes and messy brown hair, the same smile that people always said Claudia shared. She and her mother hugged, and it felt wonderful.

In school on Monday there was a big rehearsal for the Harriet Tubman play. Claudia stood at the side of the room, watching all the action, until finally it was time for her meager part.

"Yeah, and we're not kidding!" she finally got to say, and then she sat down. She watched as Stephanie Hunt stood up front and acted; Stephanie put a lot of feeling into the part of Harriet.

If only I were given a chance like that, thought Claudia. Somehow she wanted to find a way to be noticed. People got noticed for different reasons. They discovered a cure for a disease and won the Nobel Prize, or else they committed some terrible and famous crime. Or else they just tried to *look* noticeable, like Danger, whose hair fell into her face so you couldn't see her eyes, and you were always wondering what she looked like underneath all that hair. Molly Harding was famous, too. And people paid attention to Claudia's mother, but only because Claudia's father had left home. People in the building liked to be nosy when things were going badly.

How can *I* ever have people notice me? Claudia wondered. At eleven Claudia had no idea of what she wanted to do with her life. Some kids knew already what they wanted to do and were burning to be master chefs, or fire fighters, or zoologists. Stephanie Hunt was destined to be an actress.

Claudia had absolutely no idea what she would end up doing. "Relax," her mother said. "You have at least another ten years to decide."

But if she knew now, maybe she could become more interesting. Maybe people would start to notice her, would say, "Oh, there goes Claudia Lemmon, the girl who wants to be an astronaut." She would always have something interesting to talk about.

"Yes," she would say, "I'm drinking a lot of Tang

these days, just like the astronauts, in preparation for the day when I can go up on a moon launch. Let me show you my antigravity chamber."

One of the rooms in the apartment would have no gravity, and guests could walk on the walls and ceiling.

But frankly, space did not call to her. She had no great desire to put on a helmet and bulky suit. It was enough to wear her giant down coat each winter morning and look like a girl made of pillows.

The only thing unusual about her, she knew, was her dream life. And it *was* a whole life. The world became interesting and scary and exciting once every nine nights, and it just made her friendship with Danger all the more solid.

If it weren't for the dreams, Claudia knew, they probably wouldn't be friends. Danger would think she was boring and babyish. Claudia would think Danger was a showoff and a phony. But it was the strange coincidence of their dreams that brought them together. What was the point? Claudia sometimes wondered. Why had they been given this power? There had to be a purpose, she felt, but she couldn't think what it could be. All she could do was wait.

The next day after school they decided to go up to Dr. Byrd's floor and look around the hall. Together they rode the elevator up to the penthouse. In the hallway there was a small table with a vase of dried flowers on it. The hall was calm and quiet. There were two doors. One of them had a brass plaque that read: "EDNA BYRD, M.D." The other door was blank.

Claudia and Danger waited there for ten minutes, their ears pressed against the door, but they didn't hear a thing.

"Let's go," whispered Claudia. "Nothing's happening."

But all of a sudden they heard footsteps, and the other door swung open. Out walked a young woman, and she was sobbing into a handkerchief. Luckily she was crying so hard that she didn't even notice Claudia and Danger. She just rang for the elevator and got in.

"See?" hissed Danger when the woman was gone. "I *knew* something was up. She must have been torturing that poor woman. What else could it be?"

Claudia thought hard. The case against Dr. Byrd was getting stronger. "I just don't know," she said slowly. "I just don't know."

The next afternoon was Wednesday, and Claudia and Danger went to watch a Little League baseball game in the park.

They sat in the bleachers in the sun. The day was

warm and quiet; it was so nice not to be in school, Claudia thought.

"Claudia?" asked Danger. "Remember when you told me about your father and I sort of blew you off?"

"Yes?" said Claudia.

"Well," said Danger, "I'm sorry about it. Spending time with you lately, I see that I was wrong. It's unusual—I'm almost never wrong—but I guess your father's disappearance *is* a mystery. Your mother is so nice and pretty, and you're not a bratty kid. How could he have left?"

"Thanks, Danger," Claudia said, and she meant it. She smiled up into the sun and thought about her father. She pictured his face and his bald head and his favorite green-and-blue-striped tie.

"I always thought my parents were happy," said Claudia. "My mother insists that they were, although she also says that my father was always a little sad. He felt unfulfilled. He's always lived in big cities, and he really wanted to live a life where he could play his guitar all day and become a country-western legend."

"Why couldn't he just watch *Hee Haw* on television?" Danger asked.

"It wasn't enough, I guess," said Claudia. She looked up at the bright sky over the playing field. "I just don't understand how he could leave everything like that," she said, "and not even let us know where he is or how he is doing. On my mom's birthday we thought maybe he would call or send a card, but *nothing.*"

"Did you file a missing persons report with the police?" asked Danger.

"No," said Claudia. "My mother said she wasn't going to chase him. It was his choice to leave. He said, 'Come with me,' but my mother told him she didn't want to leave. He's probably living by himself in an apartment somewhere, singing in a bar at night."

"What's your father's name?" asked Danger.

It was an odd question. Her father had always been *Dad*, nothing more. "Murray Lemmon," Claudia said.

"Maybe he has a new stage name," said Danger. "Like Murray-Bob McCoy."

"Or Billy Dean Lemmon," said Claudia.

"Or Slim Jim Murray," said Danger.

They were getting silly, and they started to laugh. Claudia began to feel less sad. They made up a few more stupid names, and then they turned their attention back to the baseball game. It was the beginning of the ninth inning, and the bases were loaded.

5 °∘

One afternoon Claudia came home and heard a strange voice in the apartment. Her mother was giving another English lesson, and this time the student was a man. His name was Leon Chang, and he was from Peking, China. He was a handsome man with a warm smile and a neatly pressed blue shirt, and he shook Claudia's hand very hard when they met.

"Your mother has been teaching me American slang," said Mr. Chang. He looked at his watch. "My lesson is over for today. I'd better hit the road, Jack, and swing by my own pad to get some grub."

After he had left, Claudia and her mother cooked dinner together. It felt nice to stand side by side in the bright kitchen, peeling carrots and chopping onions.

"I'm so happy with my job," said her mother. "Not only is the pay all right, but I also get to meet such interesting people. Miss Neruda taught me a yoga exercise that's good for the spine, and Miss Tobler, my Swiss pupil, yodeled for me at the end of the lesson. Mr. Chang said he would write up a recipe for Peking noodles when his English gets good enough."

Claudia and her mother sat down at the table with a big pot of fragrant stew between them. "Mom?" said Claudia. "Do you think about Dad a lot?"

Her mother looked down at her plate. "Oh, sometimes," she said. "I try to distract myself as much as I can."

"Me, too," said Claudia. The dreams were certainly distracting her. She could think of little else.

It had occurred to Danger and Claudia that the dreams were like a handbook, giving information every step of the way. They would have to learn to be patient, in order to figure out what to do next.

The next afternoon Claudia and Danger were sitting in Danger's room when there was a knock on the door. "Mindy," called her mother, "would you mind helping me dry some prints? I have a lot to do, and I'm in a big hurry."

"Oh, okay, Mom," said Danger, rolling her eyes. She and Claudia got up and followed Danger's mother down the long hall that led to the studio. Danger looked annoyed that she had to help out, but Claudia was curious. She had always wanted to see what the studio looked like inside.

"All right, girls," said Danger's mother. "Why don't you come with me into the darkroom?"

She led the way into a small room that was, appropriately, very dark. One small pink light was glowing in a corner. It took Claudia a minute to realize that Danger's father was in the room. After a while she could make out Mr. Roth's broad back and dark hair. He was leaning over a machine, squinting into it.

"Hi," he said, turning around. "Claudia, have you ever been in a darkroom before?" he asked.

"No," she said. Mr. Roth had barely said one word to her since she and Danger had become friends. Both of Danger's parents were always very busy and never paid much attention to anything but their work.

Now Danger's father was giving her a tour of the darkroom. He showed her how the enlarger worked, and he let her peer at an image as it grew bigger and bigger just by his turning a knob. Claudia's favorite thing in the darkroom was the chemical bath. Mr.

Roth put a blank piece of paper into a tray of smelly chemicals, and in a few seconds a picture began to appear. Finally Claudia could see that it was a naked baby lying on a white rug, smiling.

"Good," said Mr. Roth. "I'm sure Mrs. Havisham will be very pleased with this photo of her son Norman."

Claudia felt nervous and pleased as she stood in the darkroom.

"Do you have any interest in photography?" he asked Claudia.

"A little," she said, and suddenly it was true. She did have an interest. She wanted to learn how to make photographs appear like magic.

"Well, if you ever want a quick lesson and my wife and I are free, just be sure to holler," said Mr. Roth.

"Thanks," said Claudia.

"Hey, come on over here, Claudia," Danger called, and Claudia went to see what she wanted. Danger was standing over something that she called a drum. It was a big roller, and she was rolling prints around and around on it until they were dry.

"You can help if you'd like," said Danger's mother.

Claudia dried prints for a while, and she kept thinking how wonderful it would be to have parents who were photographers, parents who worked together and liked it.

Danger's household was very different from Claudia's, but there was one similarity: Both girls were only children. Neither of them had brothers or sisters to spend time with, and so they needed friends more. Both of them had grown up primarily around adults.

Finally Claudia looked at her watch and realized that it was dinnertime, and she needed to get home.

"See you later, Danger," she said.

All three Roths said goodbye to Claudia in unison.

The next dream surprised her. There was very little mystery to it. She was sitting with Danger in a small, bright room, and in walked Claudia's father.

"Hi there," he said. "Sorry I've been away for so long, but there have been things I just had to do."

"Where do you live now?" Claudia asked him.

"Oh, that's a secret," he said. "I can't reveal that information."

"Why not?" Claudia asked.

"Well," he said, "if I told you where I was living, that wouldn't leave anything for you to figure out, now would it?"

"No, I guess not," said Claudia.

"I've got to go," he said finally. "Sorry to be so brief. But I'll see you again soon, I hope." Then he was gone.

The encounter had been very unemotional, Claudia thought after she woke up. She hadn't even jumped up to hug her father. She hadn't called him Dad or even cried at all. Yet the dream felt very real to her. It certainly was her father. He was wearing his favorite green-and-blue-striped tie, and his bald head shone.

Before school that morning Danger and Claudia met in the lobby downstairs. "I'm glad you're here," said Danger. "It was a strange dream, wasn't it?"

"No," said Claudia. "Not really."

"Well, maybe we had entirely different dreams," said Danger. "Maybe we counted wrong, and last night wasn't the ninth night."

Claudia quickly counted on her fingers. "No," she said. "We counted right. Tell me your dream."

"Okay," said Danger. "Here goes: You and I were sitting in a little room, and in walked this strange man. I just sat there, and you and the man had a big conversation. I couldn't make out what you were talking about. He looked familiar to me in some way, but I really couldn't place him. I kept thinking he was someone I had seen on TV."

"What was he wearing?" Claudia asked, just to check.

"I think he had on a weird tie with stripes," said Danger.

Claudia was excited. "Danger," she said, "something serious is definitely going on here."

"Did you have the same dream?" asked Danger.

"Yes," said Claudia, "with a twist. That man was my *father.*"

Neither of them spoke for a long time. Finally Danger let out a breath. "Wow!" she said. "I thought he looked familiar. But why do you suppose I thought I had seen him on TV?"

Claudia smiled. "You did," she said. "There's a photograph of him *on the TV* in my living room."

Claudia told Danger what her father had said in the dream. "It doesn't make a whole lot of sense," said Claudia. "The dream was very matter-of-fact, as though it had only been a day since I had seen him, not nine months."

"It's been *nine* months?" asked Danger.

"That's right," said Claudia.

"Hmmm," said Danger. "We have the dreams every nine nights, and you dream about your father nine months after he leaves. It sounds like the number nine is pretty significant."

It was getting late. Claudia knew she would have to run to school now to get there on time. "Look, I've got to go, Danger," she said, "but why don't you come over after school today? We can talk about it more then and fill out the dream book."

Danger agreed, and they went their separate ways. As Claudia raced to school, her satchel swinging against her, she thought about how complicated her life had become in the last few weeks. There was so much going on in her head each day; she could barely keep track of it all. They still hadn't figured out the story of Dr. Byrd and the dream about the waiting room, and now there was *this* confusing dream. She didn't know which one to focus on first.

In school that day Stephanie Hunt sat down next

to Claudia during lunch. The cafeteria was very noisy. A food fight was taking place across the room, and oranges were being flung back and forth.

"You know, I never get to see you anymore," said Stephanie. "I thought we were friends."

"I've been busy," said Claudia. "And so have you, with the Harriet Tubman play and all."

"Still," said Stephanie, "we used to be good friends. We used to do a lot of things together. Then you changed, as soon as your father moved out. It's been a long time, Claudia. In the beginning I thought you needed a while to be by yourself and be with your mother, but now it's almost a year later, and you still haven't returned to normal."

"It's been nine months," said Claudia quietly. "And I don't know if I ever will return to normal."

"Well, fine," said Stephanie. "Just go on being stuck-up, Claudia Lemmon. See if I care." Then she stood and moved her tray to another table.

Claudia sat by herself. She almost burst into tears but stopped herself. She didn't want anyone to see her cry. Why was it so hard for her to be friends with anyone but Danger? she wondered. Maybe it was because she and Danger had something important to take care of first. The only trouble was that Claudia didn't know exactly what it was they were supposed to take care of.

"I think," announced Danger one afternoon, "that we are supposed to find your father."

"But how?" said Claudia. "The dream didn't give us any clues to where he is."

"Well, let's examine it carefully," said Danger. "We both agree that he was in a small room. Does that mean anything to you?"

"No," said Claudia. "I can think of a million small rooms. Phone booths, closets, bathrooms. It could be anywhere in the world." But still, she liked the idea of the dream leading them to her father. Could it be possible? she wondered. Could a dream be a map?

They went over the dream again and again and finally agreed that it didn't contain enough information to get them anywhere.

"Maybe there will be a follow-up," said Danger. "Part Two of that dream. You never know."

Claudia was impatient during the lapse between this dream and the next. In the meantime, she plotted ways to get into Dr. Byrd's office and have a look around. She wondered if maybe she could sneak a passkey away from Frank, the doorman. It didn't seem likely.

On the ninth night Claudia had a dream that went beyond her expectations. There was her father again, back in the same small room. This time she was alone with him. They sat facing each other, and once again Claudia begged him to tell her where he was living.

"I'm sorry," he said. "I just can't do that. You'll have to figure it out for yourself."

In the distance Claudia could hear someone banging on a wall or door, but she ignored it and asked her father more questions.

"Don't you want to come live with me and Mom again?" she asked.

He smiled and adjusted his tie. "That might be nice," he said, "but I don't think it's the life for me."

Claudia still didn't burst into tears. She continued to sit there, facing her father, and finally she stood up. "When will I see you again?" she asked.

"In nine days," he said, and then he swiveled his chair away from her. The conversation was over.

Claudia woke up troubled. How could he be so cool to her? He was her father after all, the only one she had. He was very different in the dreams from the way he had been in real life. In real life Murray Lemmon was always telling jokes or playing tricks on people that Claudia's mother said were infantile but that still made her laugh. There was the incident of the plastic vomit found on the carpet of the living room, which at first sight was blamed on poor Cupcake, the dog. It turned out that Claudia's father had bought it for $1.69 at a novelty shop nearby.

At other times Claudia's father could be very serious, even sad. He would tell her stories from his childhood. They would sit together on the living room couch, and he would transport her back to Brooklyn in the 1950s.

"There were six of us living in the tiny apartment," he would say, and she would lie back against the big pillows on the couch. "There was me and my brother, Rudy, and my sister Shirley and my other sister, Letty, and, of course, both our parents. We also had a big dog named Scooter. I used to pretend that Scooter was a horse," her father would say, "and I would try to ride him around the living room. He would run away from me, of course, and hide under a bed."

"Tell me more, Dad," Claudia would say.

"Oh, Claudia, I've got to get up at six A.M. to sell insurance," he would say, but if she pleaded hard enough, he would give in. "Well, let's see what else I can tell you," he would say. "Oh, yes, the movies. That's an important part of this story. On Saturday afternoons my mother would give me and my brother and sisters enough money to go to the movies. It was very different from the movies of today. You would pay a low price and then go inside and watch all day. They showed cartoons, and a newsreel, and something called a serial, all before the main feature."

"What's a cereal?" Claudia asked, imagining a giant bowl of Rice Krispies on the screen.

"It's a short movie that continues each week," he answered. "My favorite was a serial called *Johnny Bronco*. It was all about a man who wants to be a cowboy, but he lives in the city and works in a bank. Sometimes, when he is dozing off at work, he is magically transported to the Old West, where he becomes a cowboy. Each week they showed a different adventure. It was wonderful! I liked the cartoons and the newsreel and even the main feature, but I lived for Johnny Bronco."

○
○ ○

When Claudia discussed the new dream with Danger that afternoon, she found that Danger had had an entirely different sort of dream from hers.

"I was standing in a hallway," said Danger, "pounding on a door. I'm not sure what sort of room it was, but all I knew was that I really wanted to get inside. When I woke up this morning, I was pounding on the headboard of my bed."

Claudia thought about it. She was getting to be as perceptive about figuring out the dreams as Danger was. "I know," Claudia said. "Remember I told you that I heard pounding in my dream? I must have been hearing *you* on the outside of the door. I guess I needed to be alone with my father for a while. I think that's why you couldn't come in."

"I bet you're right," said Danger.

They were sitting in Claudia's bedroom. Cupcake was lying on the bed between them, hoping that someone would scratch his belly, but both girls were too involved in their conversation to think about anything else.

"How much do you *really* want to find your father?" asked Danger.

"A lot," said Claudia. "I just want to see him

again. He doesn't even have to come and live with us. I just want to *see* him."

Danger propped her head up on her hand, and her hair fell in her face in the usual way. "I think we'd better do something to speed up the process," she said. "This could take years! Decades! We might be still having these dreams when we're old women. We'll have to live in the same apartment building then, so we can tell each other the dreams every day."

Claudia imagined herself and Danger tottering outside every day with canes, helping each other along the sidewalk. "We-e-ell," Claudia would say in an old, crackling voice, "tell me your dream, Danger. Was it about your great-grandchildren again?"

It was a funny thought, but it also troubled her. What if they never did find her father? What if years kept passing and he never showed up? He wouldn't know anything about her anymore, such as what grade she was going into, or who her best friend was, or even what she looked like.

"How can we speed up the process?" Claudia asked. She was reminded of those films that are sometimes shown in school, the ones that feature the speeded-up growth of a flower, from bud to full bloom.

"I don't know," said Danger. "But there has to be a way."

They were both silent for a while, just thinking. Finally Danger said, "What about a private eye?"

"A what?" said Claudia.

"You know, a private eye, a detective," said Danger. "Someone who does this professionally."

"Where are we going to find one?" asked Claudia.

"How about the Yellow Pages?" asked Danger.

They leaped off the bed and went into the hall closet, where Claudia's mother stored the telephone books. Claudia brought down a copy of the Yellow Pages from the highest shelf, and she and Danger sat on the floor with the book open between them. First they looked under "Detective." Nothing. Then "Private Detective." Nothing. Then "Private Eye." Nothing. Then "Eye, Private." Still nothing.

"This is getting exasperating," said Claudia, but she had one final idea. She turned to "Private Investigator," a phrase she had heard on TV once, and sure enough, there was a long list of names.

They decided to call the first one listed. It was a man named Dudley Arrow. His office was all the way downtown. Claudia and Danger went into the master bedroom to make the call. Claudia's mother was busy giving an English lesson in the living room; they could hear her patient voice wafting through the wall.

Danger made the call. She held the phone to her ear and said, "Dudley Arrow, please." There was a pause. "I've got to hold on," Danger whispered to Claudia. "A secretary answered. Sounds kind of posh." In about three minutes Dudley Arrow himself got on the telephone. "Hello, Mr. Arrow," Danger said. "My friend and I are inquiring about your service as private investigator." She was making her voice sound as adult as possible. "Yes?" she said. "Yes? . . . Good. . . . Tomorrow at four. . . . Excellent. See you then." She hung up.

"So quick?" said Claudia. "He didn't ask any questions about the case?"

"He said he doesn't discuss secret matters over the telephone because you never know if it's being bugged," said Danger. "But we've got ourselves an appointment, that's the important part!"

"Tomorrow at four?" said Claudia. "What will I tell my mother?"

"Tell her you're at my place," said Danger. "We'll be back by dinnertime."

They decided not to mention the dreams to Dudley Arrow. They would just tell him about the disappearance, and nothing more. The next afternoon at three-thirty Claudia and Danger sneaked out of the building and ducked into the subway station down the block. Claudia had never ridden the subway without either of her parents around. Sometimes her father used to take her to Chinatown for lunch, and they would stuff themselves with noodles, then ride back uptown together, happily bloated and content from the meal.

Now she and Danger got on the train casually and

took seats. Danger had Dudley Arrow's address written down on a tiny scrap of paper, and they rode the train all the way down to West Fourth Street. The train was crowded with an assortment of people: old men, young men, old women, babies, a Brownie troop on its way to the zoo, and a stern-faced policeman standing by the doors. The train rattled through tunnels, and Claudia and Danger sat next to each other, not saying a word.

Finally Claudia said, "Do you think this is a good idea, Danger?"

Danger paused. "Yes," she said in a measured voice. "I think so. If it's not, what do we have to lose? It's a free visit."

Dudley Arrow's office was on a small side street that took a long time to find. They rang the buzzer several times, and finally someone upstairs buzzed back. The building was old and creepy, and even Danger looked a little nervous as she stepped inside.

6

Dudley Arrow's office was a mess. There were stacks of paper everywhere and even a couple of old socks lying around. A crooked painting of the Eiffel Tower hung over the desk, and a cat was fast asleep in the middle of the floor.

"Come on in," Dudley Arrow said, stepping forward. "Just clear away a few inches of space, and sit down."

Claudia and Danger looked around and finally found two chairs. They removed some old fruit and a baseball glove and sat down hesitantly. What was even more surprising than the office was Dudley Arrow himself. He was a young man with a long, drooping mustache. He wore his hair in a ponytail in the back. He looked like a leftover hippie.

"Now, what can I do for you girls?" he asked.

Danger was the spokeswoman. She cleared her throat. "I'm Danger Roth," she said, "and this is Claudia Lemmon. We are trying to find Claudia's father, who flew the coop just over nine months ago."

Danger and Claudia told the story of Claudia's father, constantly interrupting each other and adding information. Dudley Arrow listened closely, taking notes on a piece of rumpled paper that he found on his desk.

"Hmmmm," he said when finally they were through. "We see a lot of this sort of thing. People going through mid-life crisis and deserting the family."

"Can you give us any statistics?" asked Danger.

"Oh, off the top of my head," said Dudley Arrow, "I'd say that for every eighteen thousand three hundred seventy marriages, at least twenty-eight-point-two percent end like that, for no apparent reason."

"Have you been a private investigator for a long time?" asked Claudia.

Dudley Arrow looked embarrassed. "Actually," he said, "I have to confess something to you girls. This is only my second case. And I made up those statistics about marriage to impress you. I just graduated from college last June. I've always wanted to be a private eye."

"How much will it cost?" Danger asked. "We're only in sixth grade and don't have a lot of money."

"That's negotiable," said Dudley Arrow. "Usually I think the best way to do it is to have you pay me in the end, after I've found the missing person. And if I don't find him, then you don't owe me anything. But if I do," he said, "and I fully expect to, then you owe me a hundred dollars. Does that sound fair?"

A hundred dollars! Claudia thought. How could they ever pay that? But Danger was agreeing, was saying that a hundred dollars seemed reasonable.

It would be a lot cheaper just to file a missing persons report with the police, Claudia knew, but then she would have to get her mother involved, and her mother didn't want to look for her father. This was the only way.

Just then the telephone rang, and Dudley Arrow picked it up. "Hello," he said in a snooty woman's voice. "Dudley Arrow's office. May I help you?"

That must have been the voice that had answered the telephone when Danger called the other day! Dudley Arrow had pretended to be a secretary, so people would think he had a classy office. Danger and Claudia stifled a giggle.

"Well," said Dudley Arrow when he got off the telephone, "I'm going to make my preliminary investigation this week. Why don't you girls check back with me next Wednesday?"

They agreed, shook hands, and left. When they were out in the hall again, Claudia said, "Danger, where do you expect to get a hundred dollars? Neither of us has that kind of money."

"Relax," said Danger. "In my school there are plenty of kids who could scrape up a hundred clams for me as a favor. I've written so many of their book reports for them that they owe me, and they know it."

It was getting late, and Claudia knew she had to get home soon, or her mother would begin to worry. She and Danger rode the subway back uptown, and all during the ride Claudia kept thinking about her father. What would it be like if she actually found him? she wondered. What would she say to him? Would he look different? What if he had a new girlfriend and a whole new life? She imagined him living in a trailer park in Nashville. She would come to the door of his trailer and knock, and in a minute a young blond woman would open the door.

"I'd like to speak to Murray Lemmon," Claudia would say.

"Murray-Bob!" the woman would call. "It's fer you!"

In a minute Claudia's father would come out, and he would be wearing a big cowboy hat and cowboy outfit, plus his old favorite blue and green tie.

Claudia couldn't take the fantasy any further than that. She had no idea what she would say to her father if she found him. All she knew was that she wanted to find him.

That night at dinner Claudia's mother seemed distracted. She overcooked the chicken, but Claudia didn't complain. Her mother was far away but still in a good mood.

"I had the most wonderful day," her mother said. "Miss Neruda thinks I am very limber and has suggested a yoga class that I might want to take. And Mr. Chang really makes me laugh. I haven't laughed in a long time," she said.

Claudia realized that this was true. Her mother used to have the most lovely, throaty laugh. Claudia's father would tell his stupid jokes, and Claudia's mother would throw back her head and laugh. Claudia hadn't heard that sound in months.

After dinner she and her mother played Monopoly. They set it up on the floor in the living room, and they played for three hours. Her mother won the game. Claudia wound up in jail.

"I'm kind of tired," Claudia said. "I think I'll go to bed, Mom."

"All right, honey," said her mother. They cleaned up the game together, putting the play money back into the box, and then Claudia went into her room for the night.

She sat on her bed and pulled the dream book out from under the mattress. She looked through it for the millionth time, hoping that something that she hadn't thought of before would occur to her. She looked at the first picture and read about the teenage sea and the four-eyed monster. She looked at the second picture and read about the waiting room and the scary nurse. On the third page there was a picture of a girl carrying a bowl of Jell-O onto an airplane. Then there were the recent dreams about her father. Claudia felt as if she were looking over a series of old family snapshots; the dreams were very familiar to her.

There were hundreds of blank pages left in the big pink book, and Claudia wondered how many of them would end up being filled by the time the dreams stopped. *If* they ever stopped, she thought. They might go on and on forever.

On the next dream night Claudia had a dream that made no sense. She and her father and Danger were floating on a cloud in the air. There was no talking, just floating. At the very end of the dream her father turned to her and said, "This should help you find me."

It turned out that Danger had had the exact same dream. "It was so simple and light," Danger said. "Almost religious." Claudia agreed; the dream had had the feeling of a magical fantasy. She could have stayed on that cloud forever. She and Danger had a good time drawing the picture of the cloud in the dream book. They spent a long time making it look just right.

The following Wednesday Danger and Claudia

called Dudley Arrow from Danger's parents' bedroom. "Hello," answered the snooty pseudosecretary.

"Hi, Mr. Arrow, I know it's you," said Danger. "This is Danger Roth. I was wondering if you had found out any information about Claudia's father."

Claudia sat next to the phone, straining to listen. She was still too shy to speak to him by herself.

"Mmhmm," Danger said. "I see. Very good." She grabbed a pencil and a piece of paper and wrote down something that made no sense.

"What is it?" Claudia hissed. "What's he saying?"

Danger held up her hand, signaling for Claudia to be patient. In a few minutes Danger was through. "Well," she said, "I think we're on to something."

"Tell me," said Claudia.

Danger took a deep breath. "He's located your father right here in the city," she said. "He hasn't been able to speak to him personally, but he's done some investigating and found out that he lives in Queens now, in a place called Rolling Meadows. It's some kind of hotel that sounds ritzy to me."

"Can we go there now?" asked Claudia.

"I think you should figure out exactly what you want to say to him first," said Danger.

"I don't need to figure it out," said Claudia. "I already know."

"Tell me," said Danger.

"I just want to come up to him and say, 'Dad, it's me!' And then we'll hug really hard."

"And?" said Danger.

"What do you mean, 'and'?" asked Claudia. "Whatever happens happens."

"Claudia," said Danger, "I just think you should give this some thought. I'm worried that you think your father is going to want to come back home with you and that everything will be all right again."

"That's not what I think," said Claudia, but all that night, as she lay in bed, she wondered if maybe it was true. Maybe she did secretly expect her father to see her and be so moved that he would leave his new life and come back home. He would leave his gigantic suite of rooms and his butler and maid and travel back with Claudia and Danger to his real home, where he belonged.

The next day, after school had let out, Claudia and Danger met in front of the apartment building and sneaked onto the subway once again. This time they were heading all the way out to Queens. Claudia was so nervous that she kept pacing up and down in the subway car.

"Hey, sit down, relax," said Danger.

"I can't," said Claudia.

"You've got to," said Danger. "You don't want to be a nervous wreck when you see your father, do you?"

"No," said Claudia. "I guess not." She plunked

down in her seat and looked out the window into the darkness of the subway tunnel.

Finally they got off the train and walked up the stairs into daylight. They were in a small, quiet neighborhood where the houses were close together and children were playing catch in the street.

"Want to play?" a boy called out to them as they passed.

"No, thanks!" yelled Danger. "We're on a mission!"

She and Claudia studied the directions that Dudley Arrow had dictated over the telephone. "We're supposed to make a right here," said Danger, "and keep walking until we get to a row of pine trees."

They walked along the street, and their pace began to get faster. Even Danger seemed excited. After they had found the pine trees, they came to a big iron gate. Across the top, in wrought-iron letters, was written "ROLLING MEADOWS."

"Wow!" said Danger. "He *lives* here?"

Behind the gates was a mansion. True, it was not in the greatest shape, but still it was a mansion. There was a circular driveway and a big, sloping lawn. The mansion itself was made of stone and had stained-glass windows. Vines were growing everywhere. Claudia and Danger approached the house cautiously. They walked up the wide stone steps and knocked on the heavy wooden door. In a minute a man appeared. He was very tall and thin.

"Yes?" he asked. "May I help you?"

"Uh, we're looking for Murray Lemmon," said Danger. "Does he live here?"

"Mr. Lemmon certainly does," said the man. "But I'm afraid you can't see him today. It's too late. Come back tomorrow." Then he gently shut the door in their faces.

"Come back tomorrow!" said Claudia. "I feel like we're in that scene in *The Wizard of Oz* where they finally get to the Emerald City and are told they can't go in!"

"We'll find a way," said Danger. "Don't worry."

Rolling Meadows was a very weird place. Claudia wondered how her father had managed to end up here.

"Look," said Danger, "I don't think he locked the door. I think we might be able to sneak in."

Sure enough, after a few minutes had gone by, Danger tried the doorknob, and the door inched open. She quickly peered inside. "There's no one around," she whispered. "Come on."

Danger and Claudia tiptoed inside. They found themselves in a great hall paneled in dark wood. They could hear a fountain gurgling somewhere in the distance. In front of them was a big red-carpeted staircase.

"He's got to be up there, "Danger whispered, and the two girls quickly ran up the stairs.

At the top they found themselves in another hall-way. There were rooms on either side of the hall, and the rooms had names on the doors. "It's like a dormitory for rich people," said Claudia.

They walked along the hall, reading names. Esther Smythe. Bill McCallister. John Samsa. Helen Lamar. Gary Pynchon. Finally, at the very end of the hall, they found it. There were the words "Murray Lemmon" written neatly on a card and taped to an oak door.

"This is it," whispered Claudia. Her heart was racing now. What was her father doing in this place? Had he gotten amnesia or something? She wanted desperately to take him home.

"Go on, knock," whispered Danger.

Claudia lifted her hand and knocked very lightly. There was a long pause, and finally she heard, "Come in."

In one burst of bravery she flung open the door. Facing her, sitting in a chair by a window, was Murray Lemmon, but it was not the right Murray Lemmon. This was a little old man with white hair and glasses. Claudia felt like crying.

"I suppose you're Murray Lemmon," she said.

"Yes," said the man. "Who are you?"

"I'm Claudia Lemmon," she answered, and then she burst into tears.

"Hey, hey," said the man, slowly standing up. "What's wrong, young lady?"

Danger stepped forward. "You see," she said, "my friend here is very upset because she's looking for

75

her father, who is also named Murray Lemmon, and she thought you were him."

The man smiled. "Sit down," he said. "I haven't had a visitor in months. My last visitor was a slimy fellow from a cemetery, wanting me to 'reserve space early,' as he put it."

"What sort of place *is* Rolling Meadows?" asked Danger. Claudia was still crying.

"Don't you know?" asked the man. "It's a nursing home. An old-age home. A place where you get sent when you don't have anywhere else to go and you can't take care of yourself."

Claudia looked up, shocked. "We thought it was a mansion," she said. "We thought my father must have suddenly gotten very rich or something."

"Well, this place is pretty expensive," said Murray Lemmon. "My children all chipped in to put me here. It's all right; the food reminds me of camp."

"You went to camp?" Danger said.

"Of course," Murray Lemmon said, smiling. "Camp Beaverwood, 1907. I loved every minute of it, except for the food."

Danger and Claudia were silent, trying to imagine this old man as a little boy at camp. Claudia pictured him in a bunk at night, listening to sounds outside. Now he did the same thing each night, she thought. He probably felt the same kind of homesickness.

"Can I give you something to eat?" Murray Lemmon asked.

"Okay," said Danger.

He stood up and made his way over to his bureau. From the top drawer he removed a bag of cookies and handed them to Danger and Claudia. The cookies tasted stale, but still, they ate a couple, just to be polite. They all sat in the tiny room, and the sky outside the window began to get dim. From somewhere down the hall they could hear somebody sigh.

"We've got to be going," said Claudia.

She and Danger stood up, and Murray Lemmon continued to sit in his chair.

"Lovely to meet you girls," he said. "I hope you'll come back and visit me sometime."

"We will," said Claudia, but she wondered if it was true.

7.

"**Y**ou said you had found him!" yelled Danger into the telephone. "We're not paying!"

Claudia sat and listened to Danger yell at Dudley Arrow. In a few minutes Danger was done, and she hung up the telephone.

"There," said Danger. "It feels good to yell."

"What did he say?" asked Claudia.

"He apologized," said Danger. "He said he'd get right back on the case, and he's sorry for the inconvenience."

They were sitting in Claudia's mother's bedroom. Again they could hear her give a lesson in the living room. This time she was teaching Leon Chang. They seemed to be having a good time; every few seconds peals of laughter came from the living room.

"I wish school was that much fun for me," muttered Danger.

School was a total bore these days for both girls. Claudia could barely concentrate.

"Claudia, is everything okay at home?" Miss Bernstein asked one day.

"Yes," said Claudia. "Fine."

"Because if you ever want to talk . . ." Miss Bernstein said, and her voice trailed off.

What good would it do to talk? Claudia thought. All she really wanted to do was find her father.

"Thanks," Claudia said, and then she said, "Is that all?"

Miss Bernstein looked disappointed. "Yes," she said, "that's all."

Claudia was doing badly in school for the first time in her life. Pretty soon Miss Bernstein would want to have a parent-teacher conference, and that would be awful. Claudia's mother would have to come to school, and it would be very embarrassing. But how was Claudia expected to get straight A's while searching for her father? There weren't enough hours in the day. Even sleep had become work. Every ninth night Claudia's dreams made her feel exhausted, as though she had run some sort of mental marathon.

One afternoon Danger asked Claudia if she wanted to come over and have a photography lesson. Mr. Roth had offered to teach them both.

Claudia was excited; she remembered how much she had liked being in the darkroom and watching pictures magically appear. She went over to the Roths' apartment and walked down the long hall into the studio. Mrs. Roth was taking pictures of a fat red-haired girl in a white party dress. The girl seemed very disagreeable.

"Are we almost finished?" the girl said. "I'm hungry."

"In a little while," said Mrs. Roth.

"I'm thirsty!" said the girl.

"Please be patient," said Mrs. Roth, adjusting the lens of her camera. "Your mother wants a roll of pictures as a surprise present for your grandparents."

"I hate my mother," muttered the girl.

"Okay, let's take a break," said Mrs. Roth.

She turned and saw Claudia. "Hi, Claudia," she said, and she rolled her eyes, indicating what a hard time she was having with the red-haired brat.

Claudia smiled sympathetically; then she and Danger walked into the darkroom. Danger's father was bent over the enlarger. "Hi, girls," he said. "I'll be with you in a jiff."

Claudia imagined herself becoming a photographer. She would travel around the world, taking pictures of wild animals. She could cover the Olympics. She could be a crime photographer. It seemed like a wonderful life.]

Mr. Roth showed Claudia and Danger how to develop negatives in total darkness. He showed them how to print pictures, and he even let them make a print of their own.

"The next thing you need to do," he said, "is go out and take some photos of your own. Then you'll really enjoy it."

Claudia's father had left his old camera behind when he moved out, and Claudia knew where it was kept. The next day she took the camera out of the hall closet and found that it still had a roll of film in it. Danger used one of her parents' cameras. They decided to spend the next afternoon taking pictures in the neighborhood.

They started in Central Park. They took pictures of babies in carriages and joggers running in pairs. They took pictures of a bunch of old men playing cards. After a while they got bored and walked out into the street.

"Let's take some pictures in the building," suggested Danger. "Both of our cameras have flashbulbs."

In the lobby they took a picture of Frank, the doorman. They also took a picture of Cupcake's favorite plant. Then they went upstairs and took pictures of each other in Danger's bedroom.

"I'm bored," Danger finally said. "We're not exactly getting any first-class shots."

"What sort of shot would be first-class?" asked Claudia.

"Well, an action shot," said Danger. "Something happening, something important."

Suddenly Claudia had an idea. "What if we took a picture of Dr. Byrd?" she said. "Just for our files. Maybe her face would remind us of something in the dreams."

"Well," said Danger, "it seems vague, but why not?"

Together they rode up to the penthouse. They sat in the hallway, waiting, hoping that Dr. Byrd would come out eventually.

"What are we going to say when she comes out?" asked Claudia.

"We'll just say hi and tell her that we're doing a photo collage of all the tenants in the buiding, to decorate the lobby. You know, a kind of present for the whole building to enjoy."

"Sounds kind of phony to me," said Claudia.

Just then the door swung open, and out walked a man. He was weeping. It reminded Claudia of the woman they had seen last time. People cried when they left Dr. Byrd's torture chamber.

"Take a picture," whispered Danger. "Evidence."

Claudia and Danger lifted their cameras to their eyes and quickly snapped a picture. Their flashbulbs lit up the hall in a sudden burst of light.

"Hey!" said the man, shielding his face. "What do you think you're doing?"

"Taking a picture," Danger said casually. "Just for fun. Do you mind?"

"I certainly do," said the man. He was still crying a little.

Suddenly the other door swung open, and out walked Dr. Byrd. "What's going on here?" she asked.

"We were just taking a picture," said Danger. Claudia stood paralyzed next to her.

"You had no right to do that," said Dr. Byrd. "Now I will have to ask you to give me the film."

"I can't do that," said Danger.

"And why not?" asked Dr. Byrd.

Danger shot a quick look at Claudia. "Because," she said, "because I have valuable pictures on this roll. Photographs of the last solar eclipse."

"Well, then," said Dr. Byrd, "I wish you would leave. And please do not come up here again, disturbing my patients, or I shall have to call your parents."

Claudia pressed the elevator button, and she and Danger rode downstairs together. Claudia was deeply embarrassed.

"Don't you see?" asked Danger. "Something is definitely fishy up there. Remember the unsolved dream, Claudia."

Claudia kept forgetting the dream about the waiting room, but now that she was reminded of it, she had the most peculiar feeling.

"It just proves that she has something to hide," said Danger. "She doesn't want anyone to know that her patients leave her office in tears. I mean, she made a grown man cry. She must have elaborate torture equipment in there."

"Like whips and chains," said Claudia.

"Or a torture rack," said Danger.

"Clamps," said Claudia. She wasn't even sure of what they were, but she had heard them mentioned once in a horror movie.

"We've got two mysteries on our hands, Claudia," said Danger. "This is really serious. It isn't small potatoes anymore."

That night Claudia was in a bad mood during dinner, and she barely paid attention to what her mother was saying. When the meal was over, they stood at the sink together, washing and drying pots, and her mother suddenly turned off the water.

"Okay," her mother said. "What's up?"

"Nothing," said Claudia. She thought about how her father used to use phrases like that; he would say, "What's up?" or "What's cooking, Claudia?"

"It *isn't* nothing," said her mother. "It's something; I can tell. We never used to have secrets from each other, Claudia."

"That was before," Claudia found herself saying.

"Before what?" asked her mother.

"Before things got crazy around here," Claudia said. "Before Dad moved out."

"Oh, so that's what this is all about," said her mother. "Honey," she said, "I know things are hard. I try to make life pleasant around here, but I know you miss your father. Maybe someday soon he'll face responsibilities and get in touch with us and tell us where he is. But in the meantime, we can get along without him. My new job is helping us make ends meet, and I'm learning to be independent. I'm not going to sit around crying all day. I did that in the beginning, but no more," she said. "Your father obviously has some growing up to do. I know it hurts you, and when I see your father, I'm going to give him a piece of my mind, but until then, Claudia, it's just you and me, trying our best."

You and me and a couple of confusing dreams, thought Claudia, but she didn't dare say it aloud.

After they had cleaned up the kitchen, Claudia and her mother took Cupcake for a long walk around the neighborhood. As they walked, Claudia looked up and could see the windows of other apartments. She could see families in kitchens, eating dinner. In several apartments the windows were lit up with the blue light of television sets. Claudia remembered the way she and her mother and father would sit and watch television when dinner was through and the dishes had been washed. She would sit between them on the living room couch, and Cupcake would lie curled up on the floor at their feet. It was just a plain old family scene, but now she longed for it.

Cupcake pulled hard on his leash, yanking Claudia over to a fire hydrant. Claudia watched as he sniffed the ground, looking for a perfect spot. When he was done, they headed back home. During the walk, Claudia's mother looped her arm through Claudia's.

"Oh, we'll get by," her mother said, as if she could read Claudia's mind.

"Maybe we'll have to sell matches on the street, like the Little Match Girl," said Claudia.

"We could make a fortune," said her mother.

Claudia giggled. She liked it when she and her mother were silly together. It was windy outside, but she didn't care. She forgot her troubles for a while and walked along with her mother, stopping every few yards so Cupcake could sniff a tree.

When they got back upstairs, the telephone was ringing and ringing. Claudia dropped the leash and raced to answer it. "Hello?" she said in a breathless voice.

"Is this Claudia Lemmon?" asked a man.

"Yes," she said, "this is she." That was how her mother had always instructed her to speak on the telephone.

"This is Dudley Arrow," said the man. "Sorry to call you at night, but I've come up with some information that I know will make you happy."

"Yes?" said Claudia, and her heart began to race.

"Murray Lemmon is living right here in Manhattan," said Dudley Arrow. "Up on a Hundred and Tenth Street! This time I'm sure I've got the right man!"

Claudia scrambled to find a piece of paper to write down the address. "Thanks so much," she said. "I'll check back with you soon."

"Who was that?" her mother asked when Claudia had hung up the telephone.

"Oh, just a wrong number," said Claudia, and then she went to bed.

8

*T*his time Claudia and Danger walked to their destination. It took more than half an hour, and the wind was very strong. Claudia's scarf blew in her face when she tried to talk, so she and Danger didn't prepare for the meeting. Claudia shoved her hands deep into her pockets and tried not to be nervous.

This time the building was run-down. A couple of kids sat on the stoop, bouncing a ball. An old woman sat in the lobby. It felt good to be out of the cold.

Claudia and Danger stood warming themselves up before they rang the buzzer.

Sure enough, there were the words "MURRAY LEMMON, APT. 5E." Claudia took off her mittens and pressed a finger on the bell. In a few seconds a woman's voice answered. "Yes?" she said.

"Is Murray Lemmon there?" asked Claudia.

"Who is this?" asked the woman suspiciously.

"Uh," said Claudia, and she panicked. Suddenly she was unsure of how to introduce herself. "This is his daughter," she finally said.

"His daughter!" exclaimed the woman. "Well!" Then the buzzer sounded, and Claudia and Danger walked inside.

The hallway of the fifth floor was narrow and dark and smelled of cooking and detergent. "Phew," said Claudia, and she held her nose.

She knocked tentatively on the door of 5E, and in a second the door swung open, and Murray Lemmon stood there, saying, "Darling!"

Then there was an awful moment in which he realized that this was not his daughter. Murray Lemmon of apartment 5E was a six-foot-five-inch black man. He and Claudia stood there staring at each other sheepishly.

"Well," Claudia said, "I guess your name is Murray Lemmon, right?"

"Yes," said the man. "And your father is also named Murray Lemmon?"

"Yes," said Claudia, and then she began to cry.

Danger stepped forward and explained the story to the man while Claudia tried to stop crying.

"Look," said Murray Lemmon, "why don't you girls come in? It's stupid for you to be just standing there."

Claudia and Danger went inside. The apartment was small, but it was filled with wonderful things. There were plants in every window and big, bright pillows on the couch. "This is my girlfriend, Lenore," said Murray Lemmon. "I've always told her about my daughter, Beatrice, and how much I miss her. I always hoped that someday they would meet."

"Why don't you see your daughter?" asked Danger.

"Well, she ran away from home two years ago," said Murray Lemmon. "She went to live on the West Coast somewhere. She's seventeen," he said.

"All these missing people," said Claudia, mostly to herself. It seemed that everybody longed for somebody: She longed for her father, her father longed for a new life, Murray Lemmon of Rolling Meadows longed for company, and this Murray Lemmon longed for his runaway daughter, Beatrice.

Claudia and Danger sat and had a cup of hot chocolate with Murray and Lenore. Lenore was a shy woman with dark eyes, who didn't say much but just held Murray Lemmon's hand.

Later, walking home in the wind, Claudia decided that this was not the way to find her father.

"No offense," she said to Dudley Arrow over the

telephone the next afternoon, "but we're not getting anywhere. We're going to have to find the real Murray Lemmon on our own."

Dudley Arrow was apologetic and begged Claudia to give him another chance, but she would not budge. "I'm really sorry," she said, "but I'm getting impatient. I've got to find another way to locate my dad."

"And what is that going to be?" asked Danger after Claudia had hung up.

"Through the dreams, I guess," said Claudia. If the dreams really were a map, then they ought to lead Claudia and Danger to the right place. She wished that she could speed up the nine-day process, but she knew that she would have to wait it out.

On the next dream night Claudia went to bed with a great sense of anticipation. It took her a long time to fall asleep. She kept turning and turning, rearranging the blankets and the pillow, until finally, around midnight, she managed to drift off.

The dream was an explosion of sound. Claudia and Danger were standing in a gigantic, screaming crowd. Some of the people were waving pennants. "Where are we?" she kept asking Danger, but Danger didn't know.

Suddenly an announcer spoke over the loudspeaker. "Ladies and gentlemen," he said, "the race is about to begin."

Then a shotgun went off, and six racers were out on the track. But these were not horses, nor were they ordinary race cars. The jockeys were riding giant spheres. They rolled around and around the track on their huge, flat discs, and the crowd cheered them on.

"Look!" exclaimed Danger, peering through a pair of binoculars that she just happened to have in her schoolbag. "There's a familiar face!"

Claudia was about to grab the binoculars away from Danger, when all of a sudden her alarm clock sounded, waking her from this exciting dream. She slammed her hand down on the top of the clock, silencing it. How disappointing! For a few minutes Claudia continued to lie in the dark room, her heart still pounding.

Then she got out of bed and went into the kitchen. Her mother was sitting at the table, drinking coffee and correcting a student paper.

"Good morning, honey," said her mother. "Sleep well?"

"Fine," said Claudia. She grabbed an English muffin and quickly swallowed down a glass of orange juice. She was anxious to see Danger before school. She just had to know what Danger had dreamed. "I've got to go, Mom," she said. "I want to get to school early today, to start my science project." She didn't like lying to her mother, but there was no other choice.

Her mother looked bewildered but didn't try to stop her. Claudia rode the elevator upstairs and knocked on the Roths' door. Mrs. Roth answered. "You're up early, Claudia," she said.

"Uh, yeah," said Claudia. "Is Danger around?"

"Go on in," said Mrs. Roth.

Claudia raced down the hall to Danger's room and went in without knocking. The room was still dark, and Danger was lying in bed, her hands behind her head.

"You up yet?" asked Claudia, sitting down on the side of the bed.

Danger yawned. "Yeah," she said. "I figured it was you. Nobody else would knock on our door at seven in the morning."

"Well, you know what I'm here for," said Claudia. "I could hardly wait to talk to you."

Danger sat up in bed and rubbed her eyes. "Okay," she said. "Shoot."

Claudia told Danger her dream, trying hard to remember all the details. When she was through, Danger said, "Once again, Claudia, I've dreamed Part Two of your dream."

"You're kidding," said Claudia. "Tell me everything."

"I'll try," said Danger. "My mind's still fuzzy from sleep." She yawned again, then said, "We were still at the racetrack, and I handed you the binoculars so you could look at your father, who was one of the jockeys. I remember that the number on the back of his shirt was nine-nine-nine."

"Those nines again," said Claudia. "Let's make a chart after school and try to figure it out."

Just then Mrs. Roth banged on the door. "Get a

move on, Mindy," she said. "You can't afford to be late again, or you'll get detention."

Claudia and Danger agreed to meet at Claudia's apartment after school had let out. All day, as usual, Claudia could think of nothing but the dream. In the afternoon her group was performing the Harriet Tubman play for the entire class, and everything went smoothly until it was time for Claudia's one big line. She was deep in thought about finding her father, and she forgot to speak. Stephanie Hunt kept poking her and saying, "Ahem!" but Claudia didn't listen. There was a long, embarrassing pause, and finally Claudia came out of her trance and realized that the entire class was staring at her.

"I'm sorry!" she blurted out. "Oh, what's the line? Oh yes," she said. "'Yeah, and we're not kidding!'" Then she ran from the classroom, ashamed of herself. She could hear the other kids laughing as she left the room.

Out in the hallway Claudia stood and leaned against the cool, smooth wall. What a fool she had made of herself! She and Danger just *had* to figure out where Claudia's father was, or else Claudia would never be able to pay attention in class again. The dreams had changed her life; she used to be a straight-A student, and now she was distracted all the time and on the verge of flunking.

After school Claudia raced home and met Danger in front of the building. They rode upstairs together and let themselves into Claudia's apartment. They took some milk and Twinkies from the kitchen and locked themselves in Claudia's bedroom with the dream book. They could hear the drone of an English lesson coming from the living room.

"Okay," said Danger, as they sat facing each other, cross-legged, on the bed. "Let's write down what we know so far about all the Murray Lemmon dreams."

She took out a green Magic Marker, and Claudia took out a red one. Together they wrote the following:

WHAT WE KNOW SO FAR

Small room
Claudia's father floating on the air
Jockeys racing on giant spheres (??!!?)
Number 999

"Well," said Claudia, when they had finished the list, "how is that going to get us anywhere? It's just as confusing as ever."

"Have faith," said Danger. "We'll figure it out. Now look, Claudia," she said. "Let's name all the different kinds of small rooms we can think of."

"Phone booths," said Claudia.

"Bathrooms," said Danger.

"Closets," said Claudia.

After that they were at a standstill. "Okay," said Danger. "Let's put that aside for the moment and go on to the next information."

"That would be the dream about my father floating on the air," said Claudia.

"Maybe he's become a pilot," said Danger. "We could contact the Air Force."

But that didn't sound to Claudia like her father. She and Danger sat in silence for a few minutes. "Okay," conceded Claudia. "Let's go on to the next dream."

She thought about last night's dream and the strange race she had watched. It was so odd to imagine her father participating in something vaguely athletic. It wasn't like him at all. He would certainly never have become a jockey in real life; besides, he wasn't short enough.

Claudia closed her eyes and pictured her father in a riding outfit, going around and around the racetrack on that big sphere, that disc. Suddenly a thought occurred to her.

"I've got it!" she shouted, her finger in the air.

Danger was startled; *she* was usually the one to figure out the meaning of the dreams.

"He was riding on a *disc*!" said Claudia. "He's a *disc jockey*! He couldn't make it as a singer, so he wound up as a deejay!" She was practically shouting now.

"I'm impressed," said Danger. "Really impressed. You might just be right."

"And," Claudia went on in her moment of triumph, "that cloud dream meant that he was *on the*

air. He's a deejay on the air. Don't you see? It was all pointing us in that direction!"

"What about the nines?" asked Danger. "Where do they fit in?"

"Let's see," said Claudia. "Maybe it's an address."

"Or a telephone number," said Danger.

"Or a *radio station*," said Claudia.

Both girls sat and looked at each other.

"Put on the radio," Danger said quietly. Claudia got up and brought her tiny transistor over to the bed. She moved the dial to 99.9. There was a sudden loud twang of music.

> Oh, carry me home [moaned a singer],
> And never shall I roam.
> Just want a plate of grits
> And a pair of shoes that fits.
> Just want a nice soft bed
> And a place to rest my head.

The song droned to an end, and then a man with a thick southern accent said, "This is station WDUH, ninety-nine-point-nine on your dial, bringing you the very best in country music. I'm Buzz MacAllister, and this is the request hour. Call in to 999-9999, and we'll play your favorites in country music. Oh, is there someone on the line?" he asked.

A woman's voice boomed out, "Buzz, I just *love* your show," she said. "Could you please send a song out to my sweetheart, Big Al? The song is 'Lookin' for Mary on the Prairie.'"

"Sure can," said Buzz MacAllister. In a second the song came on.

"Let's call and talk to him," said Danger. "He'll know how to get in touch with your father, assuming we're on the right track."

"Good idea," said Claudia. They went down the hall and into her mother's bedroom. Without thinking, Claudia picked up the telephone and dialed. She was met with a loud busy signal. She called back eight more times, and finally, on the ninth try, she got through.

"This is Buzz MacAllister," the deejay said. "You're on the air."

Claudia froze. Her voice was going to be broadcast everywhere! "Uh," she said, "uh, I'm trying to locate the deejay Murray Lemmon. Do you know where I could find him?"

There was a pause. "That's the first nonmusical request we've had all day on our request show," said Buzz MacAllister. "But I think you may be looking for *Hank* Lemmon, honey. He's the only Lemmon deejay who we have workin' for us here at ninety-nine-point-nine. He's got the dawn show Saturday mornings. You might want to try him then. In the meantime," he said, "can I play a little song for the little lady?"

Claudia tried desperately to think of a country and western song. She remembered one that her father had always loved. "Can you play 'Cowhand from the Rio Grande'?" she asked.

"Sure can!" said Buzz MacAllister, and in a second a blast of music came through the receiver. Claudia hung up.

"Saturday at dawn," Claudia muttered.

"Well, we'd better go to sleep early on Friday night," said Danger.

"What if it's not him?" asked Claudia.

"I just have a feeling it is," said Danger. "And that was excellent detective work, Claudia. You put Dudley Arrow to shame."

There wasn't anything left to do that day; both girls were exhausted from what they had already accomplished. They sat finishing their milk and Twinkies, and neither of them said anything for the longest time.

9

It was Danger's idea to go to the radio station at dawn on Saturday. She had looked up the address in the telephone book and found that it was located in midtown. Claudia and Danger pooled their money so they could take a taxi, and they met in the lobby of the apartment building at 5:00 A.M. The doorman eyed them suspiciously.

"Where are you girls going all alone?" he asked.

"Out," Danger said, and then she and Claudia walked out into the still-dark street.

"I've never been up at this hour," Claudia said. The city looked beautiful; she could see small lights winking in the distance, and everything was very peaceful.

They found a taxi in a little while, and Danger told the driver the address. "How did you manage to sneak out?" Danger asked Claudia.

"I was very quiet," said Claudia. "I left my mom a note that said I went for a walk with you, in case she happens to wake up and find me gone."

"Good thinking," said Danger. "I left a note that said I was out on a special mission."

The taxi pulled up in front of a plain office building. "This is it," said Danger. "I sure hope we've found him this time, Claudia."

They rode upstairs in an elevator to the ninth floor (naturally), where the radio station was located. There was a guard asleep at the front desk, so they just tiptoed right past him. A sign on the wall read, "STUDIO A," with an arrow pointing down the hall. "Let's try that one," whispered Danger.

They tiptoed down the hall until they found Studio A. A red sign was lit up that read, "ON THE AIR," but Danger and Claudia poked their heads in anyway.

Inside the studio was a blond woman sitting behind glass. "Yes," she was saying into a microphone. "Sometimes people *do* have problems like that. I suggest that you sit down and discuss it with your husband. It's always best to talk things over."

"Thank you," came a voice over the air. "You've been very helpful."

"I'm glad," said the blond woman, and then she pressed a button. "Good morning," she said into her microphone. "This is Dr. Shelly Bannister, bringing you *Loveline,* WDUH's on-the-air advice column."

"Hi there, Dr. B," came a woman's voice. "This is Darlene."

"Hello, Darlene," said Dr. Bannister in her smooth voice.

"Well, this here's my problem," said Darlene. "My boyfriend is a rodeo star, and he's always out on the road. I don't get to spend nearly as much time with him as I'd like, yet I don't want to hinder his career. Do you think I should mention this problem to him?"

Claudia and Danger were getting very involved in the woman's problem. After Dr. Bannister finished her show, they closed the door so they could try to find Claudia's father.

"We'd better go find Studio B," said Danger.

They crept down the hall and quietly opened the door of Studio B, which also had a sign outside that read, "ON THE AIR." There, sitting at a table and facing away from them, sat a man. Claudia couldn't see his face, but she could see that he had a full head of hair. This couldn't be her father; her father was *bald.* She was so disappointed that she almost burst into tears.

But all of a sudden the man swiveled around in his swivel chair, and Claudia found herself face-to-face with her very own father, the real Murray Lemmon. He was wearing a toupee on his head, but otherwise he looked exactly the same. He had on his favorite blue-and-green-striped tie.

There was country music playing in the background. "Claudia," her father said in a soft voice. Then he repeated it. "Claudia," he said again.

"Look, I'm going to leave you guys," said Danger, and she went outside. Immediately Claudia was reminded of the dream in which Danger was left outside the room.

Suddenly the song ended, and Claudia's father swiveled back around and spoke into his microphone. "This is Hank Lemmon," he said, "bringing you your favorite songs. Here's another one that I just know you'll love." He pressed a button, and in a second another song came on. There was a loud burst of fiddle music.

Murray Lemmon stood up then and walked over to the door. "How did you find me?" he asked her.

She looked up at him. All along she had thought she would want to throw her arms around him when she found him, but now she realized that she felt angry with him. She didn't want to hug him.

"It took me a while," she said, "but I managed."

She and her father kept staring at each other. "Look," he finally said, "the song is about to end. I've got to go put on another disc. I can take a break

103

in a few minutes. Just sit over here, and wait for me, okay?"

Claudia sat in a chair against the wall, and listened as her father talked to his early-morning audience. "This is Hank Lemmon," he said. "Now we're going to bring you an extra-long set of one of your favorite singers: John-Bob Cassidy! I'll be back with more fireside chat in about half an hour."

"Why'd you have to hurt me at the O.K. Corral?" drawled a deep baritone voice, followed by a few twangs of a guitar.

Claudia's father stood up again and came over to where she was sitting. He sat down next to her and pulled his chair forward so that they were facing each other, just as in the first Murray Lemmon dream.

"Why did you leave?" Claudia found herself asking, and once again she realized that the dream was being acted out.

"Well, I told you, Claudia, I needed to strike out on my own," said her father.

"But I'm your *daughter*," Claudia said. "Did you ever think about how I might feel?"

Her father hung his head. "I'm just a failure," he said. "I try hard, but it doesn't work. I tried to be a good father and husband, Claudia, but I kept thinking that there was something *else* out there—some exciting world of cowboys and country music."

104

"You wanted to be Johnny Bronco," Claudia said softly. She remembered the hero from the serials her father used to watch as a boy.

"Yes," said her father, surprised. "That's exactly it. I wanted a different kind of life. I grew up in the city, and I was always daydreaming about what life would be like as a cowboy. I knew that I had to find out."

"So how did you end up back here?" Claudia asked. "Back in the city?"

Her father looked embarrassed. "I went down to Nashville," he said, "and tried to get a spot on the *Grand Ole Opry*. They said I wasn't good enough yet, and I needed to practice. But somebody heard my speaking voice and said that I'd be real good for radio. They knew of an opening here at WDUH."

"So you've been here all along?" asked Claudia.

"For about five months," said her father. "I thought about calling you and your mother, but I was just too embarrassed. I didn't want you to know that I was right here, playing other people's music instead of my own."

Claudia felt her anger starting to soften. "Why the toupee, Dad?" she asked. "It looks kind of dumb."

Her father reached up and pulled the toupee off his head. "I guess you're right," he said. "It does look kind of dumb. I suppose it was part of my attempt to be another person. I figured that if I was going to leave my life, I'd better be a different guy. So I called myself Hank, and I got myself a rug for my head."

"But you're still the same," Claudia said.

"Yes," he said, sighing deeply. "I suppose I am."

Just then there was a loud banging on the door. "Hey!" called Danger. "Claudia, it's getting late. Our mothers are going to be worried about us!"

Just as in the dream, Danger was banging at the door. Claudia smiled to herself. "Look, Dad," she said, "I have to go. That's my friend Danger outside. You'll meet her soon."

Her father cleared his throat. "Well," he said, "do you think your mother might be interested in seeing me?"

Claudia's heart leaped. "Yes," she said. "I know she would." She was very excited and imagined reuniting her parents. She had seen that happen once in a TV movie.

"Well, maybe I'll stop by the apartment tonight," said her father. "If you really think she'll want to see me."

"Come at eight," said Claudia.

She hugged her father goodbye very hard and said she would see him later.

During the taxi ride home Danger kept trying to ask questions about their conversation, but Claudia didn't feel like talking. It seemed private, something that was between her and her father.

106

"I'll talk to you later," said Danger when they got back to the building. "I'll give you a call."

The sky was light, and the day was just starting. Claudia let herself into the apartment just as her mother was waking up.

"Where have you been?" asked her mother.

"Oh, out for a walk," said Claudia. "I left you a note."

Her mother looked at her with suspicion. "I don't know," she said. "You've been acting awfully strange lately."

"Well," said Claudia, "I've had things on my mind."

"Obviously," said her mother.

"What's for dinner tonight?" Claudia asked.

"I hadn't thought about it yet," said her mother. "I just woke up, honey."

"Could we have something special?" asked Claudia.

"Special?" said her mother. "We have all those leftovers from last night."

"How about a chicken?" asked Claudia. "And some broccoli with that lemon sauce you make."

"My, my," said her mother. "What a discriminating diner you're becoming."

"I'll help," said Claudia.

In the evening she and her mother stood in the kitchen cooking together. "Something's up with you," said her mother. "I just know it."

"Maybe," said Claudia. "Maybe not." She would not say a word. At eight o'clock, just as they sat down to dinner, the doorbell rang.

"Who could that be?" her mother asked. She stood up and went into the hallway. Claudia listened as her mother opened the door. There was a long moment of silence. Then she heard her mother say, "Well, well, Murray."

"I hope I'm not upsetting you too much," said Claudia's father. "Claudia thought it would be okay for me to come."

"When did you speak to Claudia?" asked her mother.

"Didn't she tell you?" said her father. "I saw her early this morning."

"Somebody has a lot of explaining to do," said Claudia's mother. "But I guess you might as well come in, Murray."

They walked into the kitchen, and Claudia pretended to be busy eating. She cut her chicken into tiny pieces. Her mother and father hovered over her, and finally she had to put her fork and knife down.

"Uh, hi, Dad," Claudia said.

She looked up. Her father was standing there with his blue and green tie on, and no toupee.

"What's going on here?" asked her mother. "How did you happen to see each other today? Will somebody please tell me what this is all about?"

"I think Claudia had better explain it," said her father, "since I'm still kind of perplexed myself."

Claudia took a deep breath. "I can't really talk about it," she said.

"And why not?" asked her mother.

"Because it's secret," said Claudia. "And it involves my friend Danger. I'd have to discuss it with her first."

"Claudia," said her mother, "you know that we've never been unfair with you, but it upsets me to hear that you've been sneaking around like this."

"I thought I had done something nice, finding Dad and having him come here," said Claudia. "I thought you'd be happy!"

There was a pause. "That's beside the point, honey," said her mother. "I still want to know how you found him. I don't like your sneaking around all the time."

"Marian," said Claudia's father, "maybe we should drop the subject for tonight. I didn't mean to start a family argument."

Claudia's mother relented. "Well, okay," she said. "Since you're here, Murray, you might as well stay and have some dinner."

Claudia smiled to herself. She watched as her father sat down in his usual chair. Her mother passed him the platter of chicken, and he served himself a big piece.

"Wonderful dinner," he said after he had eaten a few forkfuls.

Claudia looked back and forth at her mother and her father as though she were watching a Ping-Pong game. It suddenly occurred to her that they might want to be alone.

"I'm done," she announced. "I think I'll go inside and do my homework."

She slipped quietly from the table and went into her room. She had no homework to do, really. She sat with her ear pressed against the door and tried to listen to her parents' conversation. Perhaps they would work everything out, she thought. Perhaps it would all be fine. *She* would have been the one to bring her parents together again. A few years from now, sitting at a dinner party with her parents and their friends, her father would say, "And now, would everybody like to hear the story of how our wonderful daughter convinced me of what a fool I had been and brought me back home again?" Claudia would blush modestly but would finally agree to tell the story for the hundredth time.

But now she eavesdropped on the conversation in the kitchen. For a long time all she could hear was the clanking of forks and knives as her parents continued to eat.

Finally she heard her father say, "Marian, that was a terrific meal. First-rate. I'm glad that that hasn't changed."

"We still like to eat well around here, Murray, even when you're gone," said Claudia's mother.

"You know," she went on, "I doubt that I'll ever stop being angry with you."

"But, Marian," he said, "I gave you the opportunity to come with me, you and Claudia. To try to strike out on our own, traveling across the country. It would have been fun."

"It would have been a fantasy world," said Claudia's mother. "You still haven't grown up, Murray, have you?"

"Well," he said, "I guess we have different ideas of what it means to be grown-up."

"You still want to be Johnny Bronco," said her mother sadly, "and I still want a traditional family life. Nothing has changed."

"I'm sorry, Marian," said Claudia's father. "You know that I wouldn't deliberately try to hurt you or Claudia. I love you both. It's just that I need something more."

"You need to go through your adolescence now," said Claudia's mother. "Running around like a teenager, figuring out what you want to do. But in the meantime, there's a family to support and bills to pay. You never thought about that while you were gone, Murray."

"I'm sorry," Claudia's father said again. "I'm really sorry, Marian. I was going to send you some money as soon as I had cut my first record. But that never got around to happening, and I've been working as a deejay at a country-western station, playing other people's songs. I live in a tiny apartment above the station and barely have enough money to support myself these days."

"Well, it's okay," said Claudia's mother. "I've found a job, Murray. A job I love. It pays okay, too." She told Claudia's father about her job as a tutor.

"I'm impressed," he said.

"In a way, I really feel like I've grown up since you've been gone," she said. "I guess we both needed to do that. I'm working for the first time in my life, learning how to do something really valuable. I'm proud of my work," she said.

"I don't suppose," said Claudia's father, "that you would consider giving me another chance?"

Claudia froze as she heard this. She crossed her fingers and her toes.

"No," said Claudia's mother in a soft voice. "I don't think so, Murray. It's not to punish you or anything. I just think you'll always be dreaming of being a cowboy singer, and this family will never be enough. We need different things."

"I guess you're right," said Claudia's father. "I'm sorry that Claudia had to be in the middle of all this. I hope someday she'll forgive me."

"Well, that's between you two," said Claudia's mother.

And *this* conversation, Claudia realized, was between *those* two. She moved away from the door and sat down on her bed. She felt like crying, but somehow she knew that she wouldn't. In a few minutes she heard her father's footsteps coming down the hall. He was going to say good night to her. She quickly grabbed her social studies book and pretended to be deeply involved in her homework.

10 ∘°∘

The next afternoon Claudia's mother stood in the doorway of the kitchen.

"Claudia," said her mother, "I just don't like the idea of you and Danger running around and getting into trouble. I have no idea of how you found your father, but however you did it, it just isn't safe for an eleven-year-old. Your father says that you were at the radio station at dawn! That means that you were out on the streets when almost nobody was around. It's very dangerous!"

But Claudia wouldn't tell. She and Danger had promised that they wouldn't tell their parents anything. The mystery of Claudia's father may have been solved, but there was still the mystery of Dr. Byrd and the larger mystery of the dreams themselves. Where did the dreams come from? Claudia wondered. Why had she and Danger been chosen?

Claudia and Danger began to talk on the telephone more. After school Claudia would sit in the kitchen and call Danger. In the background Claudia's mother could be heard teaching English.

"Hi, Danger," Claudia said. "It's me."

"Hi, Claudia," said Danger. "What's happening in the four-eyed monster house?"

Claudia smiled. She hadn't heard that expression in a long time. "Nothing much," she said glumly. "Everything is terrible. I bring my mother and father together, and they decide that they don't want to get back together again."

"Parents are impossible," said Danger. "But listen," she said, "if it's any consolation, guess what tonight is?"

Claudia thought for a moment and then realized that tonight was indeed a dream night. She wondered if the magic had worn off. The mystery of Dr. Byrd still wasn't solved, but maybe, Claudia thought, it never would be. Maybe she would go to sleep and dream of something totally boring and unrelated.

"I don't know, Danger," she said. "I've sort of lost

interest in the whole thing. Look where it's gotten me."

"Claudia!" said Danger. "You can't lose interest now! We still have work to do. Those dreams were given to us like a magic power."

"Oh, Danger," said Claudia, "you've just read too many books about witchcraft and superstition and the occult. I'm not so sure I believe in any of this."

"How can you say that?" asked Danger. "Look where it's gotten us. We found your father, didn't we?"

"Yes," said Claudia, "but he didn't end up coming back to live with me and my mother. Nothing has changed."

"Yes, it has," said Danger. "You understand something more than you did before. You got to sit down and talk with your father. It was important. Maybe the dreams don't work miracles, Claudia, but I still think they're important. We met each other that way, didn't we? And we helped save Molly Harding from the hijacking."

"But look where it's gotten *me*," said Claudia. "Before I met you, Danger, I was a good student. Now I do terribly in school. I think you may be a bad influence on me."

"Well!" said Danger. "I can't believe you're saying this, Claudia. After all we've been through together."

"Oh, come off it, Danger," said Claudia. "Your name isn't really Danger. It's Mindy Mindy Mindy Mindy!"

"I think you've said enough for now," said Danger in an icy voice. "I don't want to talk to you anymore today."

"Well, goodbye then," said Claudia, and she hung up.

Claudia sat on the edge of the bed and put her head in her hands. She had ruined the one good friendship she had. Everything was going terribly.

That night after dinner Claudia and her mother took Cupcake for a long walk. They didn't talk at all; instead, they looked everywhere but at each other. It was a little warmer outside than it had been in a long time. The worst of winter was over.

They got home, and Claudia's mother hung Cupcake's leash over the doorknob of the den.

"I guess I'll go to sleep," said Claudia.

"Good night, dear," said her mother. She looked very unhappy as she kissed Claudia good night.

Claudia went into her room and got into bed. She had forgotten that it was a dream night. All she could think about was her father, and her fight with Danger. She fell asleep with all these thoughts tumbling about in her head.

It was 3:00 A.M. when Claudia woke up with a start. "We've got to help her!" she shouted. It took her a moment to realize that she had been having a nightmare. Her heart was racing, and she felt as though she were out of breath. She sat up in bed and turned on the light. Everything looked okay. There was her dresser and her mirror and her chair with all the clothing piled on it. The room was safe.

Her dream had terrified her. She had dreamed that she was snooping around the penthouse and heard screams coming from inside Dr. Byrd's office. The screams sounded like a young girl. Claudia had tried both doors, but they were locked. She didn't know what to do. She had shouted back, "We've got to help her!" hoping that someone might hear her, and then she had woken up.

The dream seemed significant. It was her turn to keep the dream book, and she got out of bed and rummaged around in her desk until she found it. Claudia turned on her small desk light and recorded the dream in neat letters. Underneath it she drew a small picture of herself in the hallway, pounding on the doors.

Claudia sat at her desk and looked out across the sleeping city. Only crazy people were up at this hour, she thought, or else poets, or night watchmen, or kids who wrote in dream books. She wondered then if Danger was awake. She felt a slight twinge and realized that she missed Danger terribly. My ex-best friend, she thought. She so much wanted to know what Danger's dream had been. She wanted to rush downstairs in the morning and meet Danger in the lobby of the building. "Tell me everything," she would say, and she and Danger would exchange dreams the way two ordinary friends might relay the plots of the TV shows they had watched the night before.

But in the morning Claudia got up and got dressed groggily. She sat at breakfast with her math book open in front of her. She dawdled with her food so that she would not have to bump into Danger in the elevator or the lobby.

"You'll be home right after school?" her mother said.

"Yes," said Claudia sullenly.

She packed her schoolbag and set off for the day. Down in the lobby there was no sign of Danger. Claudia walked around the block and bumped into Stephanie Hunt and Brian Farnham.

"Hi," said Claudia.

"Hi," said Stephanie.

"What have you been up to, Claudia?" asked Brian.

Claudia had made a stir in school after she had run out of the room during the Harriet Tubman play. Everybody was curious about what had happened.

"I've had a lot of things on my mind," said Claudia. "I'm sorry I wrecked the play, Stephanie."

"Oh, that's okay," said Stephanie. "You didn't wreck it, Claudia. At least everybody paid attention."

"My mind was elsewhere," said Claudia. "But now I'm back. I'm going to start paying attention again."

"Want to come to a party next Friday?" asked

Stephanie. "My mom says I can have some kids over."

"I'd love to," she said.

That day in school Miss Bernstein gave the class a pop quiz in geography, and Claudia thought she did very well. She even raised her hand to answer several questions during math hour. At lunchtime she sat at a big table full of chattering kids. Every once in a while she would think about Danger and the dream she had had last night, but she would quickly push the thoughts out of her mind.

After school Claudia walked home with Stephanie and Brian and then went right upstairs by herself. In the living room she could hear her mother's patient voice lecturing to a student. She stood in the hallway for a minute and listened. Something sounded a little different. Her mother, she realized, was laughing as she spoke.

"Oh, that's a good one," her mother was saying, and then her voice broke into laughter. "But if you really want the English to be correct, then you have to say, 'Why *did* the chicken cross the road?'—not 'Why *do* the chicken cross the road?' But otherwise, it's very funny, Leon."

Claudia peered into the room. Her mother was sitting on the couch next to Leon Chang. As usual, he was wearing a neatly pressed blue shirt.

"Hello, Claudia," said her mother, looking up.

"Hi," said Claudia.

"Hello there," said Leon Chang. "We've met before, Claudia. Do you remember?"

"Yes," said Claudia.

"Your mother is turning me into a regular American," said Leon Chang. "I've never seen such a wonderful teacher before. She should open a school in her own name: 'The Marian Lemmon Institute for American Speaking.'"

"Hardly," said Claudia's mother, but she was smiling.

"Well, I have homework to do," said Claudia.

"I've invited Leon to stay for dinner tonight," said Claudia's mother. "He has promised to cook us a real Peking meal. You love Chinese food, Claudia, so this should be a real treat."

"Great," said Claudia, with just a little bit of sarcasm in her voice.

She decided that she really needed to get back to her studying if she wanted to make up for how badly she had been doing all year. She was burying herself in her math homework when a wonderfully delicious smell wafted into her room. She sniffed the air deeply; it smelled like the most interesting food in the world.

"Claudia! Dinner!" her mother called.

Claudia had to admit that dinner was terrific. Leon Chang was standing at the stove with a white apron on. He was stirring vegetables in a big wok, and the air was sizzling.

121

"Sit down, you two," he said, and Claudia and her mother took their places at the table.

"Time for groovy grub!" he said, and Claudia and her mother exchanged amused glances.

Leon Chang explained what all the dishes were; there were cold noodles with sesame sauce, and stir-fried broccoli with oyster sauce, black bean chicken, and, for dessert, fried ice cream. Throughout the meal Leon explained how he had prepared each dish. He also kept Claudia and her mother amused with tales from his childhood in China.

"I was the youngest child out of a family of ten," said Leon. "When I was born, my older sister was so jealous that there was a new baby in the house that she tried to give me away. She would take me to the big marketplace and put a sign up reading: 'BOY FOR SALE. DOESN'T DO MUCH EXCEPT CRY.' Luckily a neighbor found us and brought us home, and my sister was sent to the rice paddy for the rest of the day."

The meal sped by. Pretty soon Claudia's mother looked at her watch and said, "Claudia, don't you think it's time for bed?"

"I guess so," said Claudia. Good nights were said all around, and Claudia went back into her room. As she was getting into her pajamas, she could still hear her mother and Leon Chang laughing in the kitchen.

She thought about the party at Stephanie Hunt's house next week. It had been a long time since she had been to a party. She wondered what she would wear. She wondered who would be there and whether or not she would have a good time. Claudia fell asleep thinking about the party and woke up in the morning feeling calm and happy. She hadn't remembered any of her dreams.

11

"*I*'m glad to see you back to your old self," said Miss Bernstein in school the next day, handing back the geography quiz. Claudia had gotten a 100 percent, and hers was the only perfect score in the class.

The weather was so warm after school that she and Stephanie went window-shopping as they walked home.

"Want to come over now?" asked Stephanie. "I think there's a good movie on TV, and my mother

124

baked some terrific pie yesterday, and there are still leftovers."

"I can't," said Claudia. "I have to go home and walk the dog."

"Well, maybe tomorrow then," said Stephanie.

Just as they were rounding the corner, Claudia saw Danger coming in their direction. She was walking between two big kids in leather jackets. Claudia recognized them from Danger's school. One of the kids was Gruber, the boy who had asked her if she wanted to play cards.

"Hey, Claude!" he yelled.

Stephanie whispered, "You *know* him?"

"Uh, sort of," said Claudia. She wished that she could have avoided saying hello, but it was too late.

Claudia and Stephanie stopped on the sidewalk to talk to Danger and her two friends. Both Gruber and the other kid, Newton, had the words "KILLER SHARKS" written across the back of their jackets.

"How you doin'?" asked Gruber.

"Fine," said Claudia. She and Danger were studiously *not* looking at each other. They both clutched their satchels to their chests.

Stephanie Hunt looked very embarrassed to be associating with two boys in leather jackets. She kept glancing at her watch. "We'd better go, Claudia," she said.

"So," said Danger, "I guess you two have been hanging out a lot together, huh? Best friends and all?"

Claudia just stood there, speechless.

"Come on, Claudia," said Stephanie, and finally Claudia let herself be pulled away.

As they continued to walk home, Stephanie said, "Who was *that*? She seemed really weird!"

"Oh, just somebody," said Claudia. Even though she was angry with Danger, she didn't want to hear anyone say bad things about her.

"Well, whoever she is," said Stephanie, "I'm glad you're not friends with her, Claudia. I would begin to think that *you* were a little weird, too."

"No, I'm totally normal," muttered Claudia. "Totally average, Stephanie. You don't have to worry."

They said goodbye under the awning of Claudia's building. "See you tomorrow," said Stephanie. "And don't forget my party next week. It should be a blast."

"I won't," said Claudia. She walked inside, and Frank, the doorman, tipped his hat to her.

"Afternoon, Miss Lemmon," he said. "Where's your sidekick?"

"Who?" asked Claudia.

"Miss Roth," said Frank.

Claudia felt a pang. "Oh, I don't know," she said. "I haven't seen her lately."

She went upstairs and let herself into the apartment. Just as she was coming in the door, the telephone began to ring. Her mother was in the middle of a lesson, so Claudia raced to answer it.

It was her father. "Hi, Claudia," he said. "I was

wondering if you wanted to have dinner with me this week. Just the two of us."

Claudia paused. "I'd like that," she said. "I'll have to check with Mom first."

"I miss you, Claudia," her father said. "I'd like to see you as much as I can. I don't want to lose you."

Claudia mumbled something about not wanting to lose him either, and then she made up an excuse to get off the telephone because if she didn't, she was afraid that she would start to cry.

Her mother agreed that Claudia could have dinner with her father, so Wednesday night he picked her up at the apartment at seven.

"Where would you like to go?" asked her father as they went downstairs together in the elevator.

"I don't care," said Claudia. "Anywhere."

They walked down Central Park West for several blocks. The snow had all melted, and Claudia could see the trees in the park. Pretty soon they would start to blossom, and the whole city would turn green again. Spring was her favorite time of year in New York City.

"How about some Italian food?" asked her father, and Claudia agreed. They went to a tiny restaurant and ate big plates of spaghetti. The walls had murals of Italy painted on them. Over Claudia's head the Leaning Tower of Pisa tilted precariously.

"I want to try to make up for the last nine months," said her father. "Even though I don't live with you and your mother, I'm still your father. I plan on acting like a father again, if you'll let me."

Claudia bent over her plate and twirled her spaghetti around and around on her fork. "Okay," she said at last, because the truth was that she did miss her father and didn't want to lose him again after she had had such a hard time finding him.

"Well, then," said her father, "why don't you fill me in on what's been happing in your life, Claudia? I'd like to hear."

Claudia took a deep breath. She still felt loyal to Danger and didn't want to reveal the story of their dreams. On the other hand, she had a strong urge to talk about what was happening between herself and Danger.

"Have you ever had a really good friend, Dad," she asked, "and suddenly the two of you stopped getting along?"

Her father nodded. "Benny Finkel," he said. "We were best friends in junior high school."

"Well, I have—I mean, I *had*—this best friend named Danger Roth."

"That's an unusual name," said her father.

"It certainly is," said Claudia. "She made it up, but she never admits to lying about anything. I think she lies all the time. It's just that her stories are so interesting that I get caught up in them and want to believe them. Her real name is Mindy."

"What are her parents like?" asked Claudia's father.

"They're nice," said Claudia, "but kind of distracted. They're photographers and are always taking pictures of babies. I guess they don't spend a lot of time with Danger."

"I think your friend probably needs some attention that she doesn't get at home," said her father. "That's why she makes up stories."

"It's not just the lying," said Claudia. "It's everything. She tries to be so tough and cool all the time. She even *smokes* sometimes. I know that she doesn't really like it, but she just needs to impress me. And I've gotten into all sorts of trouble ever since I met her. We got kind of involved in a big project," said Claudia. "And then my grades started to go down, and I botched my one line in a play in school, and then I ended up getting into a big mess."

"Claudia," interrupted her father, "why do you like this girl Danger? There must be something about her that draws you to her."

Claudia thought about it. "Despite everything," she said, "she's the most interesting friend I've ever had. She makes me think about things in ways that I never have. And we have a lot of fun together. We're so different, but it doesn't matter. We usually get along really well, but then I just got fed up with her, and now we're not friends anymore."

"And you feel bad about it," said father.

"Yeah," Claudia admitted. "I guess I do."

"Well, it sounds like it's up to you," said her father, "to make up with her. You've got to be tolerant of people's differences." He cleared his throat. "I seriously believe that, Claudia," he said.

After dinner Claudia and her father walked around the city for a long time, talking about many things. She looped her arm through his as they walked. Finally it was time for her to go home since it was a school night. He accompanied her back upstairs to the apartment.

"Hello, Murray," said Claudia's mother as they came in the door.

"Hi, Marian," said her father. Claudia stood watching this awkward exchange. It would be a long time, she knew, before her mother and father could be friends again.

Claudia's father went down the hall with Claudia before he left. "Where's that old guitar of mine?" he asked. "The one that I left here? I miss it."

Claudia took her father's old guitar out of the closet. It had sat there for more than nine months, untouched.

"I've been writing a new song," said her father, taking the instrument from its dusty case. "I haven't finished it yet," he said, "but let me know what you think." He sat down on the side of her bed and strummed a few soft chords.

> Almost a year has come and gone [he sang],
> And still our lives go on and on,
> I think of you when I'm tryin' to sleep,
> Into my dreams you always creep,

You're my little girl, my only child.
And like a pony you'll soon run wild.

Claudia thought about the song all night, even after her father left. It stayed in her head; she could still hear his husky voice and the gentle chords he played. It was a song for her, she knew, and she hoped that he finished it soon.

The next dream night surprised Claudia again. She had been trying hard to forget that any of the dreams had ever happened. Again she was awakened in the middle of the night, and this time the dream was even more terrifying than the last one. She was back in the hallway outside Dr. Byrd's office, and the same girl was screaming behind the door. Claudia tried the knob, but it was still locked. Suddenly Danger was there beside her, and the two of them made a running start toward the door and broke it down. They found themselves inside the waiting room. The screams were coming from the office, and once again Danger and Claudia broke down a door to get in. Finally they were inside Dr. Byrd's laboratory. It was a giant white room, filled with bubbling chemicals and elaborate equipment. Against one wall was a series of torture devices. At first glance the laboratory seemed to be empty, but still they could hear the girl screaming.

131

"Where do you think those screams are coming from?" Danger asked Claudia.

"I don't know," said Danger.

They wandered around the room, and finally Claudia noticed a big machine in a far corner. Lights were blinking on top, and the whole machine was quivering. The girl's cries were coming from inside the machine.

"Help!" she cried. "Help! Someone let me out!"

Claudia and Danger rushed over to the machine and tried to let the girl out, but they could not pry open the hatch. They stood there, struggling with it, when all of a sudden they heard a very calm voice behind them.

"Well, well," it said. They turned around, and there was Dr. Byrd. "Why don't you two snoops take a seat?" she said.

Claudia and Danger both were terrified, and they did as they were told. Dr. Byrd looked at her watch. "Almost ready," she said. In thirty seconds she pressed a red button on the top of the machine, and the lights stopped blinking. The machine came to a halt.

"What you are about to see is an amazing feat of science," said Dr. Byrd.

She opened the hatch of the machine with a key that she wore around her neck. "Come on out, Marianne," she said.

There was a sound of rustling, and then a tiny foot, no bigger than the foot of a doll, hesitantly appeared. It was followed by another foot, and then the whole girl appeared. She was six inches high and stood blinking in the bright light. Claudia could see that this was the girl who had been crying that other afternoon in Dr. Byrd's hallway.

"It's a success!" said Dr. Byrd. "My new machine is a hit!"

The tiny girl stood on the floor, looking up. "What's happened to me?" she asked.

Dr. Byrd bent down and scooped her up. "Don't worry about a thing, Marianne," said Dr. Byrd. "We'll take a nice man and shrink him down to your size, and the two of you can live happily ever after in a cage in my laboratory. You will have a whole new wardrobe, courtesy of Barbie and Ken. I hear she even has a new tennis outfit this year, so you can remain active."

Then Dr. Byrd turned to Claudia and Danger. "Now, girls," she said, "it's your turn."

"No! No!" screamed Claudia, and she and Danger grabbed hands and began to run back through the gleaming laboratory. To their horror, the door was locked. They stood there, pounding on the door and crying, "Help! Help! Help!"

That was when Claudia woke up. She found herself pounding on her pillow. The room was still dark. She sat up in bed and wiped the sweat from her forehead. Would these dreams plague her forever? she wondered. Would she just continue to have them for the rest of her life and be able to go on ignoring them? She was tempted to call Danger in the morning and apologize to her, but she decided against it. She had to forget about Danger and forget about the dreams.

It was just a stupid nightmare, Claudia told herself. It doesn't mean anything. Dr. Byrd is probably a nice, kindly ophthalmologist, nothing more. Just forget about the dreams, Claudia told herself. Just forget about them.

Claudia lay down again and pulled the blanket up to her chin. She would not be a prisoner of these crazy dreams. She would be a normal eleven-year-old girl. She would be a straight-A student—a little shy but always polite. She would be helpful around the house, and she would go back to being friends with the girls in school who were just like her. She would not, Claudia realized with a twinge of sadness, be special anymore.

12 °

When Claudia arrived at Stephanie Hunt's party on Friday night, the room was already filled. She could smell potato chips in the air. "Claudia!" called Stephanie, coming over to greet her. "I'm glad you could make it."

Mrs. Hunt took Claudia's wet coat. It was raining hard outside, and it felt good to be inside the warm room. The Beatles were playing on the stereo, and twelve kids were sitting around a bowl of onion dip. Allen Glasser was doing impressions.

"This is a piece of bacon," he said, and then he rolled on the floor and began to wiggle around, as though he were shriveling up in a frying pan. Everybody laughed and applauded. Claudia sat down on the couch and began to relax. There were nice kids in her class. Still, she realized, she missed Danger. That would never change.

She tried to put Danger out of her mind and focused instead on the party. Mrs. Hunt disappeared from the room, and Stephanie decided that it was time to play Mad Libs.

The game involved coming up with a series of words to be put in the blank spaces of a story. When all the blanks were filled in, one person would read the story back, and it would sound ridiculous. Claudia remembered the way a story began during a Mad Libs game the year before.

> Mrs. _____, a _____ woman,
>   *(silly name)*   *(adjective)*
> took her _____ for a walk.
>   *(noun)*

It ended up reading: "Mrs. Fingleheimer, a purple woman, took her noseplug for a walk." Everyone had laughed and laughed.

Now Stephanie went around the room, asking people to come up with words. "Give me a verb!" she demanded of Allen Glasser.

"Tickle," he said.

"Give me a noun!" Stephanie said, pointing to Claudia.

"Um, dream!" she said. It was the first word that had popped into her mind.

Stephanie went around the room and finally came back to Claudia again. This time she asked for an adjective. "Supernatural," Claudia said. The third time she went around the room, she stopped at Claudia and asked for a girl's name.

"Danger," said Claudia, without thinking.

"That's not a girl's name," said Peter Mallory.

Everybody began agreeing with him. "Come up with a real name," said Stephanie. "Come on, Claudia, you're holding up the game!"

"It is *so* a real name," said Claudia. "It's the name of a friend of mine."

"Well, it's a stupid name," said Cathy Burke.

"No, it's not," said Claudia, and she stood up. "I'm going home," she announced. "I don't care about your game anymore. You asked me for a girl's name, and I gave you one. If you don't want to use it, then I'm leaving."

She stormed out of the living room and found her coat on the rack in the hallway. Everybody stood and watched her leave. She felt acutely embarrassed, exactly the way she had felt when she ran out of the classroom during the Harriet Tubman play.

Claudia ran home, which was just around the corner. It was pouring rain outside, but she didn't care. There was something that she needed to do.

Claudia entered the building and raced right by Frank, the doorman. "Don't say hello or anything," he muttered as she ran past.

She got into the elevator and pressed 18. She remembered the first time she had gone up to Danger's apartment. It had been early in the morning, and she'd known that she needed to go there. Now she felt just as she had that morning. It was nine o'clock on Friday night, and Claudia prayed that Danger was home.

She pressed the buzzer several times. Finally she heard Danger's voice through the door. "Yeah, who is it?" Danger asked.

"It's me," said Claudia. "Your four-eyed monster friend."

The door opened a crack. Through the slit Claudia could see Danger's eye peering suspiciously at her. "What do you want?" Danger asked.

"I want to talk to you," said Claudia.

"I don't need any more lectures," said Danger. "All I've ever gotten are lectures. Since the day I was born."

"I promise I won't lecture you," said Claudia. "I just want to apologize."

The door opened wider. "You're kidding," said Danger.

"No," said Claudia, shoving her hands in her pockets. "I'm completely serious."

Danger reluctantly let Claudia in. They walked down the hall to Danger's room. It was even messier than Claudia remembered it. Her magic rocks and fossils and occult mementos were piled all over the floor and the bed.

"I was just looking through my collection," said Danger. "Sit anywhere."

Claudia pushed aside some stuff and sat down on the bed, her usual spot. Danger sat down across from her.

"Well," said Claudia, "I just needed to come here. I needed to apologize to you. I'm not even sure why. I mean, I know that I treated you badly and everything, but it's something else—something *powerful*—that made me come."

"It's the dreams," said Danger. "That's all it is, Claudia. It's taken hold of both of us, and we both know that we have to finish what we've started. It brought us together, after all. It's also torn us apart, but we're not going to let it."

"No, we're not," said Claudia, and then she and Danger leaned forward, across a sea of rocks and bottle caps and assorted treasures, and hugged really hard.

They sat together for an hour, comparing notes on their dreams. In both instances she and Danger had had the exact same dream.

"That makes it seem so *urgent*," said Danger. "I mean, it's almost as though the message of the dream were trying to come through twice as hard."

"I almost called you," said Claudia. "I just *knew* that you were having dreams, too, but I tried to fight it. I tried to put it all out of my head. I guess it didn't work," she said. "What do you think the dream means?" she asked.

Danger thought about it. "I'm not sure," she said. She squinted. "Claudia," she said, "something's coming to me. Just wait." In a second she stood up. "That shrinking machine is pretty interesting," she said. She paused. "Do you know what the word 'shrink' means?" she asked.

"*Duh*," said Claudia.

"No, I'm talking about the slang word," Danger said. "'Shrink.' It means a psychiatrist, Claudia. We were dreaming about Dr. Byrd, and she must be a psychiatrist!"

"We were so stupid," Claudia said. "We should have figured this out before. All those people who were crying," she said, "must have been Dr. Byrd's patients who were thinking about sad things. They weren't being tortured at all!"

"So why do you think Dr. Byrd appeared in our dreams?" asked Danger.

"Maybe," said Claudia, "she's the one who's making us have the dreams in the first place. I mean, she works with people's minds and everything."

"You are *brilliant*, Claudia," Danger said. "That must be it. I think Dr. Byrd is doing mind control on us. She's using us as her guinea pigs. She's behind the whole thing."

Claudia and Danger sat and looked at each other; there was a lot of tension in the air. "What now?"

asked Claudia, but she knew very well what was going to come next. They would have to go back up there, up to the penthouse to confront Dr. Byrd once and for all.

Without saying another word, Claudia and Danger got up from the bed and walked down the hall and out the door. The elevator ride seemed longer than usual; it felt as though it lasted an hour. Finally they arrived at the penthouse.

"What if she's not home?" Claudia whispered.

"Then we'll wait here," whispered Danger. "We'll wait all night if we have to."

But after knocking loudly three times, Claudia and Danger heard footsteps from inside the apartment. Claudia was scared, and she wanted to run. Danger sensed this and squeezed Claudia's hand to make her feel better.

"Who's there?" asked Dr. Byrd.

"Claudia Lemmon and Danger Roth," Danger said. "You know, we live downstairs."

In a second the door opened, and Dr. Byrd poked her head out. She had a head full of curlers. "What can I do for you girls?" she asked. "It's very late."

"We need to talk to you," said Claudia.

"Why don't you come back during my office hours?" said Dr. Byrd. "We can set up a time to talk."

"We don't want to be your patients," said Danger scornfully. "We have something we need to discuss with you. It concerns *you*, Dr. Byrd."

The doctor raised her eyebrows. "All right," she finally said. "I guess you can come in for a minute." She opened the door wider and led Claudia and Danger into the main room. It was a handsome room with bookshelves lining the walls. Claudia had never seen that many books in her life. A thick Oriental rug covered the floor. Dr. Byrd led Claudia and Danger over to a brown leather couch. When they sat down, they almost sank into the deep cushions.

"All right," said the doctor, "why don't you tell me what this is all about?"

Claudia and Danger began talking all at once, and Claudia stopped and let Danger speak first. "Dr. Byrd," said Danger, "you know *exactly* what this is all about."

"I do?" said the doctor.

"You certainly do," said Danger. "Mind control. You've done a good job on us, I must say. Our lives are ruled by those dreams."

"What are you *talking* about?" asked Dr. Byrd.

"You've been controlling our dreams," said Claudia. "Making us dream the same things at night. Giving meaning to our dreams. It was interesting at first, but now it's too much. We can't concentrate on anything else. Don't you shrinks know when to stop?"

Dr. Byrd patted the curlers on her head, making sure they were in right. "You girls," she said, "have very fanciful imaginations. I have no idea of what you're referring to—all this mind control that you keep mentioning. You know," she said, "psychiatrists aren't witch doctors, contrary to what some people think. We don't control people's minds. Nobody can do that. We just listen well. And I suggest that you girls stop and listen to each other before jumping to conclusions about things."

Claudia and Danger looked at each other sheepishly. Dr. Byrd was a harmless woman in a bathrobe and curlers. It *did* seem unlikely that she was controlling their minds. Claudia suddenly felt ridiculous. They *had* jumped to conclusions, hadn't they?

Dr. Byrd stood up then. "I'm going to say good night now," she said. "It's very late." She escorted them out.

At the doorway Danger turned and said, "We'd, uh, like to apologize to you. We didn't mean any harm."

"I know that, girls," said Dr. Byrd.

Back in the elevator Claudia and Danger rode up and down for a while because they still needed to talk.

"Well, we really bombed out that time," said Danger.

"I know," said Claudia.

"We have been getting kind of frantic about everything, I guess," said Danger.

"What else could we have done?" asked Claudia. "There really is no logical way to explain the dreams."

"I guess not," said Danger.

143

"To be continued," Claudia said as the elevator stopped on her floor. The doors slid open, and Claudia went home. When she let herself into the apartment, her mother was sitting in the living room, marking student papers.

"How was the party, honey?" her mother asked, and Claudia couldn't think of a single thing to say.

13.°

One night Claudia's mother threw an International Potluck Dinner for all her students. The apartment was filled with a variety of smells. It seemed to Claudia that almost every country in the world was represented.

An Arab woman named Miss Baroudi was demonstrating a belly dance in the middle of the room. Miss Tobler gave a yodeling lesson. Miss Neruda was doing yoga exercises in the corner, and three women were struggling to cross their legs into the lotus position.

Mr. Caron, from Paris, was giving a wine-tasting lesson. Leon Chang was in the kitchen, hacking up vegetables and chicken. Claudia went in to say hello.

"Hi there, Claudia," said Mr. Chang. "That's a boss T-shirt you have on."

Claudia stifled a giggle. "Thanks," she said. "What's for dinner?"

"I am making a traditional stir-fry," he said, "but I plan on sampling the delights from around the world. Miss Neruda has made some curry. It should be a wild and crazy taste treat!"

Claudia watched as Leon Chang chopped scallions and peppers into tiny pieces and dashed in some sesame oil. The room was steamy and fragrant. Smoke clouded the air.

Claudia felt happy that night. She stayed up later than she was usually allowed, learning how to belly dance. Her mother sat in the middle of all her budding pupils, beaming with pride. They all had learned how to speak English very well, thanks to her.

Finally Claudia felt herself growing sleepy. She said good night in seven different languages and went into her bedroom.

She lay down and fell deeply asleep, and in the morning she realized that she hadn't remembered her dreams. She counted on her fingers and realized that it had been nine nights since the last dream. Her heart sank. The dreams had stopped. She went downstairs and waited for Danger in the lobby. Finally Danger straggled out of the elevator, her hair uncombed.

"I overslept," Danger explained.

"Well," said Claudia, "what did you dream?"

Danger shook her head. "Nothing," she said. "Zilch. I slept like a baby."

"Me, too," said Claudia. "It's over."

"I know," said Danger.

Claudia felt an inexplicable sadness then. The dreams had caused a lot of trouble, yet she knew that she would miss them.

"Do you think we'll ever get them back?" she asked.

"Maybe someday," said Danger, "when we need them again, we'll *make* them come back."

Claudia thought about this and realized that Danger was probably right. They *had* needed the dreams. Nobody had controlled their minds and made them dream things; they had somehow brought it on themselves. They had played off each other, working themselves up into a frenzy. The dreams had brought them together. Claudia had been so shy and timid back then, but she had slowly changed. She wasn't afraid of the dark anymore, and she spoke up when she had something to say. Danger had changed, too, Claudia realized. In the beginning, Danger had felt the need to lie about things because her life wasn't very exciting. But then the amazing dreams had taken over.

"Danger," said Claudia, "do you think we would have ever become friends if it weren't for the dreams?"

Danger shrugged. "I don't know," she said. "I mean, we go to different schools and all. Which reminds me," she added. "I'm being kicked out of Shipwell. I was told that I no longer belong there. My mom says I'm going to your school in the fall."

"That's terrific, Danger!" said Claudia, and she meant it.

"Uh, Claudia," said Danger, "you can call me Mindy if you want. I've never really liked that name. I decided when I was seven that I was going to have an unusual name. I went through several before I finally wound up with Danger."

"What were some of your other names?" asked Claudia.

Danger looked embarrassed. "Velcro," she said. "Rhubarb. Alpha-Beta."

Claudia laughed. "I hope you never lose your imagination, Danger," she said.

"I told you that you can call me Mindy," said Danger.

Claudia shook her head. "No," she said, "I think I'll stick with Danger, if you don't mind."

"I don't mind," said Danger Roth.

F
Wol   Wolitzer, Meg
       The Dream book

DATE DUE	BORROWER'S NAME	ROOM NUMBER
SEP 19	Pamela Mauston	319
29	Jaime Huth	
NOV 28	Jamie Huth	
FEB 18	Chandra England	
APR 24	Linny Howard	317

130   87

MEDIALOG
Alexandria, Ky 41001